WIN HADLEY SPORT STORIES

A Win Hadley Sport Story

OVERTIME UPSET

BY MARK PORTER

SIMON AND SCHUSTER

New York, 1960

LIBRARY OF CONGRESS CATALOG CARD NUMBER:
60–8131
MANUFACTURED IN THE UNITED STATES OF AMERICA
BY H. WOLFF BOOK MFG. CO., INC., NEW YORK

CONTENTS

CHAPTER ONE

Looking Ahead

THE GLEAMING CLOCK above the fireplace showed precisely seven-thirty as Mrs. Ruth Hadley hurried through the living room on her way to the kitchen. As she had done every morning for the past ten years, she paused for a moment before the mantel and ran her fingers gently over the clock's burnished wood frame. Fondly she looked at the simple bronze plaque under its face, inscribed with the familiar words that meant so much to her.

To Dr. Eldon Hadley on the occasion of the tenth anniversary of his medical practice in Dixboro. Given in grateful appreciation by his friends, many of whom owe their lives to his skill.

The clock had been presented to her husband thirteen years ago. She still remembered the flush of pleasure in his face when he first saw it, and could still hear the soft, halting words of thanks as he tried to express to his many friends in Dixboro how deeply touched he was by their gesture. Dr. Hadley had never been much of a man with words. But then he didn't need them. Everyone knew and loved Dr. Hadley.

His big rambling figure, moving through the streets of Dixboro at any hour of the day or night was a familiar sight. With his broad shoulders and strong, capable hands, he seemed almost indestructible. But he wasn't.

Barely three years after the gift of the clock, Dr. Hadley had answered a sick call in the middle of the night. A farm laborer had hurt himself the day before. A French-Canadian who didn't know much English and who didn't trust hospitals, he tried to doctor himself. During the night, infection set in and his worried wife called Dr. Hadley.

It was January and bitter cold, but Dr. Hadley set out. He never returned. As he was driving to the Crawford hospital, following the ambulance he had called, a heavy car cut through an intersection without warning. The driver missed the ambulance by inches but, as he passed Dr. Hadley, he lost control and slammed into him. Miraculously the first car managed to stay upright. Dr. Hadley skidded wildly over the icy pavement, struck a culvert and flipped over twice. By the time the ambulance driver reached him, Dr. Hadley was dead.

Dr. Hadley left a comfortable house on one of Dixboro's more pleasant streets, a widow and two sons—Walter, aged fourteen and little Winfield, aged six. Her two sons became the most important things in Ruth Hadley's life. Proudly she watched both of them grow into fine, healthy youngsters. Walter, the elder, was like his mother—outgoing and talkative, but little Win was his father's image —reserved, but with a deep, quiet sense of humor and a strong sense of fair play and sportsmanship that was reflected in everything he did.

Both boys were good students and fine athletes; Walter had been a star football player in his time, but Win was the better all-around performer. Yes, Mrs. Hadley was proud of her two boys.

All of which reminded her that healthy boys were hungry boys. She wiped one last imaginary speck of dust from the face of the clock and moved on into the kitchen to start breakfast.

A few minutes later, a clatter on the front stairs told her that the boys were on their way. She turned to set the table in the cheery breakfast nook, but was stopped by her younger son as he banged his way through the swinging door into the kitchen.

"Hi, Mom!" he cried sunnily. "Real nip in the air this morning." He strode over and gave her an affectionate bear hug. "I'll take those," he said, indicating the silverware in her hand. "You finish with breakfast."

"Why don't you get the paper?" Win's mother suggested.

"Walt's doing that." Win scooped the knives and forks from her hand and walked over to the table.

"You don't say," Mrs. Hadley remarked as she went back to stirring up scrambled eggs. "What's come over him? He isn't usually so ambitious in the morning."

Win folded the napkins in place and grinned at his mother. "Mr. Hibbert put a big ad in the *Record* today. Walt said he wanted to see how it came out."

Win's brother worked as a salesman in Albert Hibbert's automobile agency—a company that hadn't been doing too well until Walt joined it the year of his graduation from Holden. But with Walt's drive and fresh ideas it had taken on new life.

Mrs. Hadley smiled as she poured the eggs into the frying pan. "You'd think he could trust them to print up a simple ad."

"Oh, you know Walt," Win said, reaching up for the glasses. "He wants to check everything himself. I guess that's why the auto agency is such a success."

"I guess so," Mrs. Hadley murmured absentmindedly. She stood looking down at the fresh loaf of bread in her hand. "Do you want toast or bread and butter with maple syrup? Aunt Martha just sent us down a can from Vermont."

"Hmmm!" Win smiled. "What do you think?"

Mrs. Hadley handed him the loaf. "Here, you cut it. I know you like your slices nice and thick." She turned back to the stove and began to fold over the eggs. "Now where's Walt?" she demanded. "The eggs are about ready."

"Then let's eat!" The kitchen door swung open and Walt came in, carrying the Monday morning edition of the *Crawford Record,* a hustling daily that not only carried news of the county seat, but had only recently extended its coverage with a special supplement devoted to the goings-on of its nearby neighbor, Dixboro. The idea for the Dixboro supplement came from William Madden, publisher of the *Record,* who hoped to increase circulation and raise advertising revenues with his new experiment. He assigned a new reporter to the beat, a man named Neal Travers. Travers was a fair all-around reporter, but he fancied himself as a sports writer, and so the major portion of the Dixboro page of the *Crawford Record* was devoted to sports news by Neal Travers.

"How'd the ad turn out?" Mrs. Hadley asked as Walt swung into his chair at the head of the table.

Walt held up the paper triumphantly. "Get a load of that!" he chortled.

TAKE ADVANTAGE OF TERRIFIC TUESDAY
TRADE-IN TRIUMPH!

Win eyed the heading critically over a plateful of eggs. "What if they want to buy on Wednesday?" he asked.

Walt threw his brother a withering glance. "Well, they can!"

"Doesn't say so."

"Sure it does. Further on down." Walt pointed an indignant finger at a paragraph in the middle of the page. "The sale goes on all week."

Win shrugged and reached for a pot of maple syrup. "You should let them know earlier," he declared. "Might lose some customers that way."

Walt put the paper away and looked at his brother scornfully. "The trouble with you," he said, "is that you're not in the market for a new car."

Win nodded cheerfully. "Yup," he agreed. "Not unless you're giving them away this week."

Mrs. Hadley decided it was time to come to the defense of her older son. "Well, I think it's a very nice ad," she declared. "I'm sure it'll sell a lot of cars." She looked at Walt questioningly. "Is there anything else in the paper today?" she asked.

"As a matter of fact," Walt said, with a mysterious smile, "there is. But you wouldn't be interested." He opened the paper and held it across the table airily. "It's just a story about your son."

"About Win?" A flush of pleasure rose in Mrs. Hadley's face as she reached out for the paper. "Why didn't you say so before?"

"Must have slipped my mind," Walt replied innocently. "It's on the Dixboro page. Neal Travers' sports column." He turned to Win with a grin of amusement. "Here comes another clipping for the scrapbook."

Win smiled. "She's got three whole books on you alone. I remember when I was a little boy Mom used to read me all your football notices. Boy, was I proud!"

"How do you think I feel about you?" Walt said admiringly "Four-letter man at Dixboro High and unanimous Conference choice for quarterback this year."

Win gulped down his milk hastily and shrugged off his brother's compliments. "Football's all finished now," he said. "We've got basketball to think about."

"I know," Walt nodded. "That's what the article says." He looked at his mother. "Find it yet?"

Mrs. Hadley folded the paper by her plate and adjusted her glasses. "Yes," she said. "It's a long piece on Dixboro's basketball chances."

"Well, let's hear it."

Mrs. Hadley cleared her throat and began reading:

DIXBORO HOOP HOPES HIGH AS SEASON DEBUT TWO WEEKS OFF

Speed to Keynote Cougar Attack

Dixboro's Varsity basketball hopefuls will meet today in the new Alumni Gym for their first workout of the new season. According to Coach Tom Joyce all starting berths are up for grabs. "Even veterans," says Coach Joyce, "will have to show me they mean business if they want to play. There won't be any holdovers on this team."

Despite Coach Joyce's traditional pre-season tough talk, this reporter expects to see at least two familiar faces in the starting line-up when the whistle blows for the opener two weeks from Wednesday. Towering

"Boots" Lohman, with his ball savvy and magic touch on rebounds ought to be a shoo-in for first-string center. And playing right along beside him will be Tony Parsons, the hustling right guard, whose inspired team play helped carry Dixboro into the Conference Tournament last year. Between them, these two returning seniors tallied an average of 15.8 points per game all last season. Anyone who wants their jobs will have to show he can do better. And I don't think there's anyone around who can.

That leaves three positions to be filled. Looking over last year's bench, here are three names to jot down on your scorecard—Matt Hughes, Dan Slade and Win Hadley.

Both Matt Hughes and Dan Slade saw considerable action last year, particularly toward the end of the season, when Tom Joyce began to rely more and more on Slade's sure scoring touch and Matt Hughes's driving, heads-up brand of basketball.

As for Win Hadley, I'm saving the best for the last. Young Hadley, sensational quarterback for the past two football seasons, didn't see too much action in basketball last year. A gridiron injury kept him sidelined during the early games. But once mended, he displayed a deft shooting skill that stands as a pretty impressive record. When you figure out the time played and total points scored, it comes out to an astounding average of a little under a point a minute.

Behind these five is a solid bench with steady operatives like Archie Campbell, Charley Bantam, Teddy Scholari, Gabby Windham and a whole flood of new faces up from the freshman ranks.

All in all, it looks like a good season for Dixboro. They have height (team average is a shade over six feet), speed, experience and, above all, the one-two scoring punch of Dan Slade and Win Hadley.

This is the kind of squad a coach dreams about, but all too seldom gets—in view of the way athletics are run in Dixboro's schools. At least two nearby towns schedule early sports training in elementary grades. Twining has a program and so does Crawford.

With their boys learning poise and sportsmanship on the courts in the eighth grade, is it any accident that Crawford has won the Conference title three years out of the last four?

It's a question that somebody in Dixboro should ask. Meanwhile, here's to Coach Tom Joyce and the Cougars—this year's best bet for the championship.

Mrs. Hadley put down the paper and sighed. "Goodness," she said, "how that man goes on. My mouth's as dry as cotton wool from all that reading. I'll have to have another cup of coffee."

"I'll get it, Mom," Win said, jumping up. "You sit still."

"Here," Walt said. "Fill up mine while you're

about it." He handed Win his cup. "What'd you think of the crystal ball act?"

Win lit the front burner and shook his head doubtfully. "I think he's taking a lot for granted. Particularly about me. I only played a few games last year. Nobody can tell much from that."

Walt tipped back in his chair and gazed thoughtfully up at the ceiling. "I'll tell you what I'll do," he said. "I'll bet you a double banana split down at the Malt Shop that you'll average at least twenty-five points a game."

Win grinned and returned to the table, carrying the cups. "You must enjoy spending money."

"No, I mean it, Win."

Win spoke quietly. "What I'd like to do more than anything else is to help the team win a championship."

"Sure, but wouldn't you like a double banana split too?"

Win grinned slowly. "I guess so. It would be a real nice way to end the season."

"First of all," Mrs. Hadley said firmly, gathering up the breakfast plates, "you've got to start the season. Neal Travers says that practice begins today. What time?"

"Three-thirty."

"Don't be late."

Win laughed. "Don't worry about that!"

CHAPTER TWO

The Challenge

"Hey, Win! Wait up!"

At the sound of feet pounding up the gravel path behind him, Win stopped and turned. The next instant, the spindly figure of "Scoop" Slocum, glasses perched at a precarious angle over the bridge of his nose, notebook clutched in one hand, skidded to a halt beside him.

"Where you headed?" Scoop asked breathlessly.

"The gym. Basketball practice starts today. Or had you forgotten?" Scoop Slocum was the sports editor of the *Dixboro Diary*, the high school newspaper. He had been writing excited articles about the new season for the past two weeks and Win knew that Scoop wouldn't be likely to slip up on the date of the first session.

Scoop grunted with satisfaction and swung into

step alongside Win. "Did you read Neal Travers' column today?" he asked.

Win nodded.

"What did you think?"

Win threw him a cautious look. "Is this for publication, Scoop?"

The reporter assured him it wasn't.

"Okay, then. I think Travers is right in one respect. The team's got great potential. I think the starting line-up he mentioned is a pretty good one —except for me."

Scoop looked at Win in astonishment. "You're kidding!"

"No, I'm not." Win paused to make his point. "Look, last year I played in exactly six games. Not much of a record, eh?"

"Yes, but look how you scored!" Scoop protested.

Win shook his head firmly. "Doesn't mean a thing. Besides, the fellows had orders to feed me the ball. All I did was to stand on the outside and dump them into the basket. That's the only thing I could do. Doc Prentice wouldn't let me move around with that knee injury. So, most of last season, while the other fellows were working together, I was down at one end of the court practicing set shots. And that," Win concluded, "was what they used me for."

"Well, how do you feel about your chances this year?"

Win smiled grimly. "I've got a lot of catching up to do, but I'm sure going to try. Don't forget," he went on, "you've got to be more than a set-shot artist to make a basketball team."

"You'll make it," Scoop said confidently.

"I hope so."

Scoop changed the subject abruptly. "Say, how about that idea of Neal Travers' to start teams back in the eighth grade? I think it's great."

"So do I," Win agreed. "But where are they going to practice? The high school gym's got a full schedule with the Varsity and J.V."

"What about the elementary school gym?"

"That's no good," Win objected. "That's for the whole school. You know as well as I do that all the kids use the elementary school gym for supervised play after school. They have volleyball and the little kids run relay races. In the winter time it's the only place for them to get exercise. You can't take a gym away from a couple of hundred kids and give it to a dozen or so. That's kind of unfair."

A strange look passed over Scoop's face. He stopped and looked around over his shoulder and leaned toward Win confidentially. "But they're going to do it just the same," he said quietly.

Win wheeled around in amazement. "What do you mean? Who is?"

"Ssssh," Scoop cautioned urgently. "Nobody's supposed to know about it yet."

"Then how come you know?"

"My Pop," Scoop explained. "He was talking about it with Dan Slade's father the other day at the Rotary lunch. He's got it all worked out."

"I don't believe it."

"Well, it's true," Scoop insisted. "It seems that Mr. Slade just hired a new bookkeeper at the saw-mill—a fellow called Joseph Harsh. Harsh found out that the whole Slade family is basketball-happy and told Mr. Slade that he used to do some coaching."

"Where?" Win demanded. "I never heard of him."

"In the army. Service teams. Anyway, they got to talking about this elementary school team idea and Harsh volunteered to teach them a few basic fundamentals—all on his own time, of course."

"What did Mr. Slade say?"

"He went crazy for the idea. Said it was exactly what Dixboro needed. He offered to give Harsh all the extra time he needed for coaching."

A puzzled frown furrowed Win's face. "You mean this is going to be the official Dixboro elementary team?"

"No, of course not. Harsh would have to get an appointment from the Board of Education for that."

"Then what makes them think they can use the elementary gym?"

Scoop plunged his hands into his pockets and stared moodily down at the ground. "That's where they're clever. Mr. Slade and a group of five or six of the most prominent men in town have called a special meeting of the Board of Education to request the use of the elementary gym for their team."

"Do you think they'll get it?"

Scoop looked at Win out of the corners of his eyes. "Mr. Slade's a member of the Board," he said quietly. "And so are two of the other men interested in the plan."

Win shook his head in amazement. "I must be dense, or something," he said, "but I still don't understand why Mr. Slade and that bunch are so keen on this idea."

"Don't you see?" Scoop said patiently. "Freddie Slade, Dan's little brother. He's in the eighth grade. So are the sons of the other men who are pushing this thing."

"Aahh," Win nodded thoughtfully. "So that's it." He paused as a fresh thought struck him. "You mean," he asked incredulously, "that the team is already picked?"

"Sure. Wasn't that obvious from the start?"

The two boys walked along in silence, with Win trying to sort out his emotions. Win finally broke the silence. "First they choose a team without holding open tryouts. Then they take away a recreation area that's used by over a hundred kids. If your father's not a friend of the insiders, you can't play. How do they expect to get away with that?"

"They will," Scoop assured him. "They've got their arguments all set. They'll say it's for the good of Dixboro. If Dixboro comes up with consistently first-rate teams, the publicity will reflect on the town. People will begin to talk about the place—maybe move their homes and businesses here. I forgot to tell you. They've got the Chamber of Commerce behind them."

"My brother's on the Chamber of Commerce," Win said grimly. "I bet he doesn't go along."

"Then he'll be in the minority," Scoop said philosophically. "Anyway," he continued, "they'll say they realize they are depriving some of the kids of recreational opportunity. But, on the other hand, it's for the ultimate benefit of everyone in Dixboro."

"Is Neal Travers behind this too?"

"He hasn't made his move yet. But he's heard rumors, and I think he'll probably go along."

"How do you feel?"

"Me?" Scoop looked at Win with surprise. "I think the idea is okay, but I don't like the way they're doing it."

"Are you going to say so?"

"In the school paper, you mean?"

Win nodded.

Scoop stopped and faced Win. "Yes, I am," he said seriously. "They'll try to stop me and I may even lose my job on the paper. But I'm going to write what I think."

"Good boy." Win reached out and grabbed Scoop's hand. "You're okay," he said warmly.

Scoop smiled shyly. "Thanks, Win. And good luck."

"What about?"

"Basketball practice." It was Scoop's turn to look innocent. "Or had you forgotten?"

Win looked at his watch. "Oh my gosh!" he cried. "It's almost three-thirty. I'll see you later."

Scoop waved him off. "I'll be up in the balcony watching."

Win tore into the locker room at a full gallop, loosening his tie as he went. The first person to greet him was Whitey Comstock, a man who had acted as a trainer for Dixboro's athletic teams for thirty years. In the eyes of most of Dixboro, Whitey was as much a part of the school as the ivy that clung to the walls.

He eyed Win quizzically from under a lanky mop of almost snow-white hair. "Been waiting for you," he announced.

"Sorry," Win breathed. "Got held up." He stripped off his jacket and yanked off his tie. "Where'd you put me this year?"

Whitey gestured to a locker near the shower room. "Same locker as always. Hurry up and dress so I can lock up and get out on the floor."

Win nodded and suited up quickly. A minute or so later, he was padding out on the hardwood floor of the new Alumni Gymnasium. The new gym was the pride of the town, with its vast, polished basketball court that looked almost the size of a football field, the latest in the way of glass backboards, and its towering tier of seats that fanned out and up from the playing area. An indoor running track ran around the second story like a balcony. Removable flooring and collapsible chairs converted that area into a second seating section if the crowd warranted it. All told, the Alumni Gym could hold a little better than three thousand people. It was an impressive plant for a small-town high school and nearly everybody in Dixboro was behind it. The sale of season tickets for all home games was running considerably ahead of expectations.

Right now, the huge barnlike interior was deserted except for about twenty-five boys, grouped around several baskets, practicing lay-up shots. The *tap-tap* of the round leather ball against the floor echoed hollowly throughout the gym. That, and the occasional shouts of encouragement from the players, were the only sounds to be heard.

Win looked around, tried to fight down the butterflies that started flapping in his stomach, and moved out to join the group under the nearest basket. He recognized Red McGinley's flaming hair and saw Charley Bantam dribbling with intense concentration toward the basket. Under a basket on the opposite side of the court he spotted Boots Lohman with a ball. Guarding him was Teddy Scholari, who was trying to make up for his lack of height by waving his arms wildly over his head.

Boots moved gracefully toward the free throw line, drawing Teddy along as if he were on a string. With a sudden, catlike motion, he broke for his left, then, in a beautifully executed maneuver, reversed his direction. Teddy, who thought Boots was going to shoot, scrambled back and leaped up to block the ball. When Boots saw that Teddy had committed himself, he brought the ball back down to his chest and shot a perfect bounce pass to Tony Parsons, who had been playing dummy over to the right of the basket. Tony had seen the play coming and was away even before Boots had fired the pass. He picked up the ball under the basket, took one step and flipped his body as he jumped for an easy lay-up. Gabby Windham, who had been guarding Tony, shook his head sheepishly; he had been caught flat-footed and he knew it.

But it was Teddy who had made the biggest blunder. He never should have left his feet on the defense. Win recognized the error and so did Teddy. He flushed and drew an angry hand across his forehead.

Win whistled softly in appreciation. The two veterans were good. There was no doubt about it. They had made their play look easy and their opponents look foolish. It was going to be tough to have to play at their level.

As he stood quietly on the side lines, absorbed by the proceedings out on the court, a deep voice grated into his ear. "Not bad, eh, hot shot? Think you can keep up?"

Win turned to find the grinning face of Dan Slade beside him. Although they were classmates and had known each other all their lives, Win and Dan were arch-rivals. Both boys were superior athletes, with Dan having a slight edge in height and weight. The only trouble with Dan was that he couldn't forget he was good. And what was even worse, he wouldn't let anybody else forget it either. Underneath, Win recognized Dan as essentially a decent sort, but with a sensitive pride and a hot head that swelled easily. At the moment the boy, strikingly handsome with his wavy blond hair and sharp-featured face, was staring at Win with a mocking smile.

Win forced himself to answer in an even voice. "Hi, Dan. They are pretty good, aren't they?"

"We're all pretty good," Dan replied. "Boots Lohman, Tony Parsons, Ed Walsh, Matt Hughes and myself." He paused to let his next words sink in. "Sounds like a strong first string to me."

Win was forced to agree. "I'd be proud to play with a bunch like that."

"We might even give you a chance to sit on the bench alongside us," Dan cracked.

Win tried to pass off the insult lightly. "Oh, I imagine we'll all get a chance to play a little," he said.

Dan suddenly turned serious. "Listen, Hadley," he said tensely. "There's something you've got to get straight. Right from the beginning."

"Oh?" Win asked.

"We're out to take the championship this year

and nobody's going to stop us. Particularly a ball-hog and fancy set-shot show-off like you."

"Like me?" Win interrupted.

"Yes, you!" Dan replied heatedly. "You got into a couple of games last year and that's all you did. Shoot and shoot and shoot."

"Some of them landed," Win pointed out.

"Sure some of them landed! If you shoot enough you're bound to hit with a few. But that's not good enough for this team. Understand?"

Win started to move away. "I think so." He was determined to keep his temper and not blow up on the very first day of practice.

But Dan wasn't finished. "And another thing," he went on. "I've got just as good an eye as you have, and I know the style of play Coach Joyce uses."

"So what does that mean?"

"It means I've got a chance of winning the Conference high-scoring title this year. I want that cup, Hadley, and you better not try to get in my way."

Win was surprised by the ferocity in Dan's tone. He had never seen him so worked up. He returned Dan's fierce gaze placidly. "All right, Dan. Good luck to you." Win took a deep breath and plunged on. "But now there's one thing *you* ought to know. I'm going to try to take that cup away from you."

Dan reared back as if he had been slapped. The color drained from his face and he took a step toward Win, his hands balled tight into fists. But before he could speak, the sharp, urgent blast of a whistle cut through the echoing sounds on the court.

Win looked around and saw Coach Tom Joyce standing at the far end of the gymnasium, a basketball tucked under his arm. He gave a second blast on his whistle and pointed to the bleacher seats along the side court. The players dropped their basketballs and trooped over.

Dan, his eyes staring stonily ahead, brushed past Win to join them. Win followed close behind, thinking to himself that the season had gotten off to an unfortunate start.

CHAPTER THREE

First Blood

WIN TRIED TO FORGET about the incident with Dan Slade as he clambered into a row of seats with his teammates. His best friend, Matt Hughes, flashed him a welcoming wink and shoved over to make room. When Matt shoved, even in a friendly fashion, something had to give. The red-haired boy with merry blue eyes tipped the scales at about 205, but there wasn't an ounce of fat on his body. A space opened up magically at Matt's left and Win lowered himself into it with a grin of thanks.

"Thought you weren't going to show up," Matt whispered. "Me and Archie Campbell here—" he gave Archie a playful nudge that nearly sent him off his seat—"we thought you got mixed up and went to football practice out of force of habit."

"I got talking to Scoop Slocum and didn't notice the time," Win murmured.

"I saw you talking to somebody else," Matt growled, throwing a black look at Dan Slade. "It looked like Little Boy Blue didn't like something you said."

"I'll tell you later," Win said. "But shut up for now. The coach wants to get going."

Coach Tom Joyce stood quietly in front of his players, waiting for the shuffling murmur to die down. When he finally had their attention, he smiled and nodded. "Glad to see so many of you here. If I've added it up right, there should be twenty-seven." He paused and bounced the ball against the floor. "That's good for me," he went on, "but not so good for some of you. I'll have lots of talent to choose from and—I may as well get the bad news over with—that means twelve of you will have to play J.V. There's room for only fifteen on the Varsity squad."

In the moment of silence that followed, Win could feel the tension mount. Some of the younger players shifted uneasily in their seats.

"As of now," Tom continued, "I don't know any of you. I'm from Missouri. You've got to show me. You've got to show me you can play ball—that you can hustle, use your heads and be flexible enough to learn an entirely new style of basketball."

A murmur of surprise went through the players. As far back as anyone could remember, Tom Joyce had always taught the same style of play—a careful brand of basketball that concentrated on defense and moved the ball up slowly in attack, waiting until the opponents made a mistake before trying a shot.

Tom didn't seem to notice the effect of his statement. He went on quietly, choosing his words with care. "I know that you're all accustomed to playing possession ball. You've all worked hard perfecting the pass patterns that go along with that kind of game. Now, I've got nothing against possession ball. As a matter of fact, as a general rule, it's the best. It sharpens up the fundamentals—the ball handling, the playmaking and all the rest of it. But every once in a while a squad comes along that combines basic basketball know-how with exceptional speed." He paused and looked the players over. "And that's the kind of squad we've got this year.

"Now," he said, putting the ball down and walking back and forth in front of them. "This means we can use a more diversified attack. We can play a wider, more open game, using the fast break and a modified zone press. We can mix up our styles and confuse the opposition. Just as they get the hang of one offense, we'll switch to another. I realize," he went on, "that this will mean extra work and hard work. But I think it'll pay off by building a championship team." He looked at them expectantly. "How about it? Any questions?"

Win saw Dan Slade's hand fly up. Tom turned to him. "Yes?"

"There's one thing I don't get." Dan's voice sounded troubled and resentful. Win suddenly realized why. Dan didn't want to change. He had told Win down on the court that he knew Tom Joyce's style and expected to win a scoring championship with it. Now if he was forced to experiment, he was afraid it would throw him off balance and injure his chances.

"What's that, Dan?" Tom asked.

"You said we were a good team, right?"

"I said I was from Missouri. You've got to show me."

"All right, then." Dan sounded more annoyed. "We've got potential, okay?" Tom nodded. "So why bother to experiment? We can probably win the Conference title with our old style. We all know it."

"And so do all the other teams in the Conference," Tom pointed out. "They're so confident we'll play the same way that they probably won't even bother scouting us. They're planning their defenses against us right now. And let me tell you something else. It's a lot stronger Conference this year than last. Too many coaches I know are going around with smug smiles on their faces."

"I still say we can take them the old way," Dan insisted.

Tom stopped in front of Dan and spoke to him earnestly. "But what about the game, Dan?" he asked. "This way, you'll learn twice as much basketball by the end of the season."

"I'm not playing to learn!" Dan exploded. "I'm playing to win!"

Tom threw Dan a hard, steady glance. "So am I, Dan. And so is everybody on the team." He walked over to the ball, picked it up and faced the others. "All right," he shouted. "On your feet. We'll loosen up a little first. Let's have four lanes and keep up some pace. I want to see some high, clean passing. And be sure you time it right for the lead."

The squad gave a yell and surged down to the court. Win grabbed a ball and dribbled over to the far side. Quickly, he lined a pass to Archie Campbell, who pivoted neatly and shot it over a slender boy that Win didn't know. The pass was short and the boy had to put on the brakes suddenly. But he flung out one hand, cupped the ball and jumped. High in the air, he snapped his body around and rocketed a clean throw to Matt who was halfway down the court. Matt took it with a grunt of surprise and heaved it to Win who was under the basket. Win drove in from the left and hooked it through the cords neatly.

Win grinned over to the slender boy and waved. "Great save, fella!" The boy grinned back.

Gabby Windham swooped down, took the ball out of bounds and rifled a short one to Archie. From Archie it went to Matt, then to Win, back to Archie, over to Gabby, downcourt to the stranger, a flip pass to Matt, who faked for the basket and then handed off to the newcomer. A graceful rim shot—and the ball settled through the hoop.

The five of them cheered and lined up for the return trip. The big gym was now a blur of action and a carnival of noise as over two dozen boys fired the round ball back and forth with whiplash precision, yelling enthusiastically for each fine play.

It was a squad workout with spirit and Win suddenly felt fired up. For the first time he was looking forward to the season with confidence. Just as he was beginning to feel really loose and relaxed, a sharp blast interrupted all play.

Coach Tom Joyce was moving out into the center court, looping a whistle around his neck. "All right, fellows," he called. "Gather 'round."

Win felt a sense of nervous expectation settle over the players as they moved into a silent semicircle around Tom. They all knew, without being told, that this was it. From here on, their moves would be watched, their mistakes noted. The weeding-out process had begun.

Tom nodded at his squad approvingly. "That's what I like to see," he said with a smile. "Lots of sparkle." He turned to one of the players up from the freshman squad. "Keep it up, Jensen. Nice work."

Win had been playing under Tom Joyce for a little over two years, and he knew some of the older man's tricks. Whenever he knew the boys were keyed up, he had a habit of congratulating someone—usually one of the younger members of the squad. It nearly always worked. Out of the corner of his eye, Win saw the gangling sophomore flush with pleasure at the compliment. The tension was broken.

"All right now," the coach went on. "We'll run over some of last year's patterns and get the kinks out of them." He turned and pointed a finger at five boys in quick succession. "I want Lohman, Parsons, Walsh, Hughes and Slade. Lining up against them, we'll start Campbell, Bantam, Windham, Scholari and McGinley. No tap-up. Lohman's team with the ball. Work it down carefully and see what you can do. The rest of you settle down in the stands and watch." He led the way off the court and continued to talk to the boys in a conversational tone. "These two teams have worked together before," he explained. "They know each other and they know the plays. I want you to get familiar with their style. It's called possession ball and it's what we used last year. Defense is strictly man to man with the player in the bucket calling the switch. All right!" he called, blasting out with his whistle. "Play ball!"

Win settled down with the rest of the rejects and tried to keep his mind on the action in front of him. He knew it was too early for it to mean anything, but he was still a little hurt that he hadn't been called for one of the two scrimmaging teams.

His face must have shown his disappointment, because, as Dan Slade walked by to take his position, he flashed Win a smirk of triumph. Then suddenly Win realized that the first team Tom Joyce had named was exactly the line-up Dan had predicted. He hunched forward grimly and concentrated on the play.

Standing out of bounds behind his own basket, Tony Parsons waited until the second team sorted itself out into a defensive alignment. When they got themselves into position, he looked over to Tom who nodded back briefly. Tony bounced the ball once, then floated a short pass to Matt Hughes.

The two forwards, Dan Slade and Ed Walsh, drifted downcourt to hover around the edges of the keyhole.

Matt moved the ball a few steps before he handed off to Boots Lohman, the towering playmaker. Boots took one step to his left and held the ball well above his head. Charley Bantam, who was covering him, had the choice of going for the ball or playing it safe. He decided on caution, and Boots was faced with the problem of finding a receiver. Matt crossed over behind him and Charley popped it back. The two boys were now in a line, about mid-court, facing the basket.

Tony Parsons spotted the setup and moved behind Matt to take the ball. That made three offensive players in a row, with a traffic jam of defense men in front of them, each trying to guard his opponent.

The moment of uncertainty was all the starting team needed. Matt and Boots broke for the basket, pivoted neatly and reversed themselves. As they fanned out down the floor, the defense men tried wildly to call the switch. Charley Bantam and Gabby Windham got completely turned around and ended up by crashing into each other. Tony saw the hole and drove past them down the middle. As the lightning-fast dribbler moved in for a certain score, both Teddy Scholari and Archie

Campbell lost their heads. Teddy deserted Dan Slade and lunged for the ball. Tony braked quickly, dodged Teddy's flying leap and rifled the ball to Dan. Smiling with satisfaction, Dan dribbled in and prepared himself for an easy jump shot.

In theory it was the right move, but he was too confident and too slow. Archie Campbell managed an unexpected burst of speed and cut to the corner to block Dan's shot. This left Ed Walsh totally unguarded underneath the basket, in perfect position to make a simple lay-up tally. Dan ignored him and followed through. At the last second, Archie's groping fingers found the ball and sent it sailing high in the air.

The players converged under the basket and got ready for the rebound scramble. But, unexpectedly, the ball wobbled to the rim, hung there for a fraction of a second and then dropped through. Dan Slade had drawn the first blood of the scrimmage.

Watching it from the side lines, Win knew it was a bad play. Dan should have passed off. The shot should never have been made, and the fact that it was a score was no excuse. The double screen that had set the play in motion was beautifully executed, but Dan had botched it by hogging the shot for himself.

A sharp blast from Tom Joyce's whistle stopped all action. The coach strode angrily to the middle of the floor. "Time!" he bellowed. "All right, Slade," he said grimly. "What's the name of your game?"

Dan flushed and stared down at the court. "How do you mean, Coach?" he mumbled.

"The rest of us are playing basketball," the coach rasped. "That's a team game. With five players on each side." He paused to let his words sink in. "Or didn't you see Walsh standing there in the clear?"

"I thought I had the shot," Dan said with a frown.

"You did," Tom Joyce snapped. "But you didn't take advantage of it soon enough. Did you expect Campbell to stand there flat-footed and wave you on into the basket?"

Dan shuffled uncomfortably. "No, sir."

"When you saw he was too quick for you, you should have passed off to Walsh."

"But I made the shot!" Dan pointed out defiantly.

"That," Coach Joyce said, turning away coldly, "has absolutely nothing to do with it."

In the uncomfortable silence that followed, a dry voice spoke from somewhere in the balcony. "I don't know about that," the speaker drawled.

"Strikes me that basketball's a game where you gotta shoot to win."

The effect of those few words was like an electric shock. There was a general gasp of astonishment from the floor. Win's head snapped around to see who had dared to walk into a practice session and disagree with the coach. To his surprise, he saw it was a stranger, flanked by ten little boys, some of whom he knew. Standing beside the stranger, looking displeased and a little embarrassed, was the bulky figure of Owen Slade, Dan Slade's powerful father.

CHAPTER FOUR

A Difference of Opinion

It was one of the most uncomfortable two or three seconds that Win ever remembered. All of Dixboro knew of Tom Joyce's strict rule about privacy at practice sessions. Scoop Slocum and Neal Travers, because of their special positions as sports writers, were the only exceptions to this cast-iron rule. All other visitors were required to check with the coach first.

In answer to the stranger's impossibly rude remark, Tom Joyce walked slowly over to the gallery and stopped quietly in front of the intruder.

"My name is Joyce," he said softly. "I don't believe we've met."

Mr. Slade shouldered his way through the gaping crowd of little boys and flashed a beaming smile. "This is Joe Harsh," he announced. "He's new in Dixboro."

Tom acknowledged the introduction with a

43

slight nod. "What can I do for you, Mr. Harsh?"

Again, before Harsh had a chance to speak for himself, Mr. Slade broke in. "Joe's my new office manager," he explained. "He sort of looks after things in town while I'm up at the sawmill."

"I see," Tom replied, obviously not seeing at all.

Mr. Slade went on doggedly. "Joe's had quite a lot of experience in basketball, Tom," he said. "Coached a few service teams." He paused and looked hopefully at Tom, but Tom maintained a disconcerting silence. Mr. Slade seemed to grow more uncomfortable. He smiled at the two men and clapped them both on the shoulder. "Joe's agreed to do Dixboro a favor. Yes, sir, a real favor. Joe's going to coach a new team. The Dixboro Midgets." Mr. Slade nodded proudly. "It'll be a team made up of youngsters from the elementary school. Isn't that something!"

Tom still refused to be impressed. "Where are they going to practice," he said dryly.

The smile faded from Mr. Slade's face. He shrugged evasively. "Well, that hasn't been decided yet, but we have a couple of ideas."

Tom nodded impassively. "Sounds like a nice idea. Good luck to you." He continued to look at the two men inquiringly. "But I still don't understand what I can do for you?"

Mr. Slade's beaming smile reappeared magically. "Oh, that!" he said. "These little fellows are just about the most eager bunch of boys you've ever seen. When they heard they were going to play basketball they were full of questions." He laughed patronizingly. "You've never seen anything like it." He lowered his voice confidingly. "We thought it would be a regular treat for them to get a glimpse of the Varsity in action. Sort of fire 'em up, you know." He dug a jovial elbow into Tom's ribs. "So you go right ahead with your practice. We'll just stay up here and watch. We wouldn't disturb you for a moment."

Tom backed away and stared at him coldly. "You already have," he said. "I believe you know the rules about practice sessions."

"Oh, sure," Mr. Slade said hastily. "Of course we do. But we thought this was a special case. We thought . . . er . . . that is . . . we were sure you wouldn't mind."

Tom looked at him bleakly. "I do," he said. "I'd appreciate it if you left. Right now."

Mr. Slade colored slightly, but kept control of his temper. "Now look, Tom," he said. "There's no need to get your fur up." He shot a black look in Harsh's direction. The newcomer had been standing quietly to one side, examining his fingernails. "I'll admit that Joe's remark wasn't the most tactful thing in the world to say, but . . ."

"This has nothing to do with Mr. Harsh or his opinions," Tom interrupted. "It's just that we have a job to do and we can't do it with visitors."

Mr. Slade tried one last approach. "Think of it this way, Tom," he appealed. "Joe here is going to be coaching boys that you'll have to work with in a year or two. Isn't it important that you two get along? You can sort of exchange views on the best way to develop players. I'm sure there'll be profit on both sides if we're allowed to stay and watch . . ."

Tom sighed, but held his ground. "You're absolutely right, Mr. Slade, but observation of Varsity practice isn't the way." He turned and gave Harsh a frosty smile. "I'll be more than happy to talk tactics with Mr. Harsh at any time. I have a genuine interest in the boys over at the elementary school."

Harsh held Tom's gaze for a moment, then shrugged and turned on his heel. "Come on, Mr. Slade," he said. "We're not wanted."

"Just a minute," Mr. Slade said sharply. "Won't you reconsider, Tom? It's for the eventual good of the school and the whole town."

"I've told you that I'll meet Mr. Harsh whenever he's ready. We can discuss plans then."

Harsh swung back and gave a short laugh. "Don't hold your breath, Joyce. You and I don't have a thing to talk about."

Mr. Slade seemed surprised at Harsh's unexpected outburst and moved in to take over the role of peacemaker. "Isn't that a bit hasty, Joe?" he said.

Harsh held his ground. "No, it isn't." He swung around to face Mr. Slade. "I've never been much for beating around the bush," he declared. "And I don't intend to start now. Your coach and I just don't play the same brand of ball."

"But you haven't seen enough to know," Mr. Slade protested.

"Oh, yes, I have," Harsh insisted. "I saw him try to curb your son on that last play. Dan had the ball and he was in basket range. So why shouldn't he shoot? Sure, I know, I know," he added hastily as he saw Mr. Slade about to break in. "It wasn't the perfect shot. But when do you get the perfect shot? Only a couple of times a game." He shook his head in disgust. "Possession ball is old-fashioned," he declared. "It's slow and it's dull. I teach a wide-open game with the kids driving for points every second. That's what I'm going to do with the Midgets and that's what's going to make them the best team in Dixboro." He finished his outburst and glared at Tom Joyce as if daring him to disagree.

Tom merely shrugged. "I think you'll do Dixboro a great disservice if you make your boys play that kind of ball." Tom kept his voice soft and his words even. "At their stage of development, they've got to learn fundamentals. If they don't, they'll grow up to be sloppy players."

Harsh grinned triumphantly. "They may be sloppy players," he said, "but at least they'll be winning players. And that," he declared, jamming his hands into his pockets, "is all that counts."

Tom stood stock-still for nearly a minute, then stepped back. "Will you go now, please?"

Mr. Slade sighed and beckoned to his charges. As they filed obediently past him, he shook his head at Tom and followed. Harsh gave Tom a veiled smile and took his place at the rear of the line. At the exit, he stopped and waved back airily to the Varsity coach.

"Don't worry, Coach!" he said. "I won't steal any of your secrets. I don't want them." He cupped his hands around his mouth and yelled down at the silent and still shocked Varsity squad. "Any of you fellows who want to come around and watch practice, you're welcome. Maybe you can pick up some pointers." He grinned boldly at Tom Joyce and disappeared.

Tom waited until the door closed, then turned back to his subdued players. If he had been upset by the incident, he didn't seem to show it. His voice and manner had the same quality and asssurance they always did. From his position in the cramped balcony seats, Win watched him with open admiration. Tom Joyce, he decided, was quite a man.

"We'll walk through that last play," Tom was saying, "and see what everybody did wrong." He held the ball out to Tony Parsons. "You passed to Matt Hughes. Right?" Tony nodded and flicked the ball over to the big left guard.

"You fellows in the bleachers watch this," Tom called out. "Matt takes the pass and moves it down his side of the court. Notice how Slade and Walsh have taken the initiative by getting down to flank the basket. Matt can't afford a pass to them. It's too long and their guards might intercept. Parsons moves up even with Hughes. That leaves Matt with two choices. He can return the ball to Tony or pass it to Lohman who's standing about five feet or so across the mid-court line. All right," Tom shouted. "Freeze!" As the players on the court held their positions, Tom walked over to the seats. "You're on the defense," he said. "Somebody tell me how you'd guard each man." Tom scanned the row of faces in front of him. "Jensen?" he suggested, calling on the boy he had complimented earlier.

Jensen swallowed once and began ticking off his moves. "I'd guard Slade and Walsh close," he said. "They're in scoring position and besides, Hughes might make a mistake and try a pass. Then I'd be set for an interception." Tom nodded and Jensen went on. "Lohman's in a dangerous spot. He's almost inside scoring range. I'd keep about two steps in front of him. If I got too close, he might go around me, but at a couple of steps I can wait to see how he'll make his move. Parsons and Hughes aren't immediate threats. I'd guard them loose. They're in no position to score, or even set up a scoring play on the next throw."

"Good," Tom said approvingly. "Now you're on the offense. You've got the ball. What do you do with it?"

"Just what Matt did," came the prompt reply. "Pass it to Lohman."

"Why?"

"No point in giving it back to Parsons. That's not getting the ball any closer to the basket."

"What if Lohman was being guarded very closely and you couldn't risk a pass? Would you give it back to Tony, then?"

Jensen bit his lip and thought about his answer. "No, sir," he said finally. "I'd keep dribbling downcourt and wait for my guard to make a move."

"What if you got in a box?"

"There's always Tony. If I got trapped, I'd know Tony could get me out of it."

Tom seemed pleased. "All right, Jensen. Go to the head of the class." He turned back to the players on the court. "Next move," he said. "Matt passes to Lohman, and Charley Bantam moves in on Boots. Boots tries to suck Charley in, but Charley's playing it cozy. Matt sees a chance for a screen play and drifts over behind Boots. Notice how that draws Red McGinley over to the center of the court. Lohman pivots, hands back to Matt and freezes. How are they going to break? The two defense men aren't sure and should step back to give themselves a little room to maneuver. But they're eager and press. That's the first mistake. Tony Parsons sees what's happened and decides to try a double screen. He moves up behind Matt and that draws his guard, Gabby Windham, over to join the party. Freeze!" Tom commanded.

"You see what we've got here," Tom continued. "Three defense men all jammed up together, practically standing on each other's shoes. The three offensive players, on the other hand, are lined up one, two, three, facing the basket, with plenty of room to try all sorts of tricks. Tony takes the ball, and Matt and Boots fake down their alleys, reverse and cross over. Now the defense players really get confused. They bump around like lady shoppers at a bargain basement sale, trying to get sorted out. Red McGinley sticks to Matt, but Charley Bantam and Gabby Windham both take off after Boots. That leaves Tony in the clear. He drives in for a jump shot and yanks Teddy Scholari out of position. Now there's nothing between Dan Slade and the basket except a couple of feet of empty court, so Tony wings one over to Dan. Archie Campbell, who's been hanging on to Ed Walsh, gets worried. He forgets all about Ed and moves out to block Dan, leaving Ed under the basket, begging for the ball. But Dan elects to take the shot. That was the only mistake made by the attacking team."

He paused and grinned over at his squad. "But that's what practice sessions are for. As you can see, possession basketball is something like a game of chess. The object is to keep pressing your attack, but with full control of the ball, until your opponents make one false move. Then you follow up your advantage with a series of plays that throws them further and further off balance until you can score. Of course, there's one big difference between basketball and chess," Tom continued. "In basketball, the play we just reviewed would take maybe fifteen seconds. That's why precision is so important in this sport. You've got to be fast and use your head at the same time. But even more than that," he added significantly, "It's a team game. One man can't do it alone."

He looked over his squad and let the words sink in. "All right," he said after a moment. "You're excused until tomorrow. In the meantime, think about what happened today."

CHAPTER FIVE

Two Coaches

"Now why," Matt Hughes said wonderingly as he prepared to dig into a Malt Shop Special later that afternoon following practice, "do you suppose the coach got rid of us so soon? We only went through one play."

Teddy Scholari, who was slumped in a chair next to Matt, sighed dejectedly. "One play was plenty," Teddy said. "I had no idea basketball was such a complicated game."

"Theodore, my boy," Matt said grandly. "You get discouraged too easy."

"Well, wouldn't you?" Teddy demanded. "I never saw a guy make so many mistakes." He shook his head ruefully. "Gee, if I keep that up, I won't even be able to make that new team Mr. Slade was talking about. What did he call it?"

"The Midgets," Win answered.

"Speaking of them," Matt said suddenly, putting down his spoon, "how do you like the idea?"

"I don't," Charley Bantam declared with unexpected bitterness. "My kid brother's in the eighth grade and he knows all about it. Freddie Slade's been bragging about the team for a week now. He says only his friends can play."

"I don't know how your brother feels about it, but I'd say he was lucky not to have to play under that Harsh fellow." This came from Gabby Windham, and from him it was practically an oration. The others looked at him in surprise. "You've got a point there," Charley conceded with a grin. "He sure wins my vote as the most unpleasant guy I've met this year."

"I'll say," Teddy agreed. "I bet Harsh and his big mouth was the reason Coach called a short practice."

Red McGinley seemed to disapprove. "He shouldn't have let it get under his skin," he said with a frown. "We need all the practice we can get."

"It depends on what kind of practice, Red," Win said thoughtfully. "I think the coach realized we were sort of knocked off base by what happened." He looked around at the circle of faces grouped at the table. "I don't know about you fellows, but I sure didn't feel up to a real tough scrimmage."

"Yeah, I see what you mean," Matt said slowly. "I guess the coach felt that analyzing that one play in depth was enough for today."

"It sure put Mr. Harsh back in his place," Teddy chimed in.

"Right," Matt agreed.

Win pushed back his chair and stood up. "I think I'll go home and hit the books," he announced. "Tomorrow's another day and I bet it'll be a tough one for all of us."

Matt gulped down the last of his ice cream and lunged to his feet. "Good idea," he said. "I'll come with you."

Win's prediction turned out to be accurate—not only for the next day, but for the next two weeks. Tom Joyce worked his squad mercilessly as he reviewed old techniques and laid the groundwork for new ones. It was pass and probe, dribble and feint, protect the ball and constantly stay alert for the first mistake. The whistle blew almost continually as Tom patiently corrected flaws and pointed out missed opportunities.

Win was happy about the pace for two reasons. First of all, he had a lot of catching up to do if he wanted to make the Varsity. There always seemed to be half a dozen new plays to be learned each day, and Win often fell asleep at night going over each move, figuring out the probable positions of every player on the court.

The second reason was Dan Slade. Dan was clearly unhappy with Tom Joyce's new style of play. He had thoroughly mastered the old attack patterns and resented any attempt to force a change. Dan was in an ugly temper, but at least his anger was directed at Tom Joyce—not at Win, whom he all but ignored. Win was grateful not to be dragged into a running feud with Dan. It kept his mind free to concentrate on learning the game.

By the middle of the second week, Win was beginning to feel a lot better about his chances. His shots were hitting and he was finding the quick openings. By Friday, he was positively enthusiastic about the team and said so to Matt Hughes and Scoop Slocum after lunch in the cafeteria.

Matt and Scoop took his comments strangely. Instead of agreeing with him, they exchanged glances and walked on without saying a word. Win waited for a reply and, when none came, he demanded to know the reason. "All I said was, I thought we had a great team. What's so bad about that?" he asked in a hurt voice.

Matt grinned and threw a huge arm around Win's shoulder. "Those are noble sentiments, my boy," Matt said. "But like the spider said to the fly, sentiment's got nothing to do with it."

"I still don't get you," Win said in a puzzled tone. "I thought we were really shaping up."

"You mean *you're* shaping up," Scoop said moodily. "I've watched practice every day and you're doing a great job. I've never seen anybody concentrate so hard."

"And that," Matt said abruptly, "is the whole trouble. You're so wrapped up in your own game that you don't see what's happening to the team."

Win stopped his friends and led them into one of the small study alcoves off the main corridor. There was a troubled look on his face as he sat them down and pulled up a chair for himself. "All right now," he said seriously. "What have I been doing wrong?"

Matt stared at Win for a moment and then shook his head sorrowfully. "Boy," he sighed. "For someone's who's supposed to be bright . . ."

Scoop made an impatient gesture and cut him off. "Don't horse around, Matt," he interrupted. "This is serious." He turned to Win and leaned forward earnestly. "Look, Win," he began in a low voice, "you're not doing a thing wrong. But there's one thing you've got to understand." Scoop was groping for words now and Win waited patiently for him to find the right ones. The young reporter moved to the edge of his chair and began to talk more rapidly. "Here's what I mean. You hardly practiced with the team all last season. Right?"

Win nodded.

"All right then; you've had a lot of homework to do. You knew it and so did everybody else. Nobody was really worried about you catching up, because you're too good an athlete . . ."

Win laughed and shook his head doubtfully. "Thanks a lot, Scoop, but I've been worried."

Scoop nodded understandingly. "That's just the point we're trying to make. You've been so worried about doing a good job yourself that you haven't had a chance to step back and take a long look at the team as a whole, if you get what I mean."

"Well, what *is* wrong with it?" Win demanded.

Scoop scratched his head and began groping after words again. "It's like one of those high-powered sport cars that should be able to do anything. Only it doesn't perform right because . . . well, because . . ."

"Because it doesn't have the right spark plugs," Matt supplied. "Or because all its cylinders aren't working properly. It's something you can feel and you know it's going to get worse."

"Can you put your finger on the trouble?" Win asked.

Matt grunted and leaned back in his chair. "Nothing easier," he announced. "Take a look at Dan Slade. He's moody and temperamental. He's not playing with the team. He takes shots from all over the court and if you ever pass him the ball, you might as well kiss it goodbye. You'll never see it again on that play."

"But I thought Dan had been playing pretty well," Win protested. "He sure racks up points in scrimmage."

"That's true," Matt admitted. "The trouble with Dan is that he's such a good player naturally, that most of his mistakes are covered up. Where he really hurts the team is on defense. He doesn't seem to care about that."

"But the worst part of all," Scoop said, "is that it's affecting other guys. He's got Ed Walsh playing the same kind of game. Even Red McGinley's been trying it."

"And don't forget the sophs," Matt added. "They don't seem to know what to do with the ball except to shoot with it."

"But that can't all be Dan's fault," Win said.

"Of course it isn't," Scoop explained. "The Varsity's got a second coach. Or hadn't you heard?"

Win looked so surprised that the other boys

broke out into grins. "Sure," Matt said. "Sir Joseph, the Harsh, the shining knight and new savior of Dixboro's basketball hopes."

"What are you talking about?" Win asked. He was genuinely surprised, because he had almost forgotten about Harsh and the project of starting a Midget team.

"Harsh still hasn't got official Board approval to use the elementary school gym. But that's just a question of time. Meanwhile, Mr. Slade talked the principal into letting the Midgets practice in the gym on Saturdays. You remember Harsh inviting the Varsity over to watch?"

"Sure."

"Well, about half the squad goes over there every Saturday morning. They hear Harsh attack Tom Joyce and his coaching methods. According to Harsh's theory of basketball, every man's a star. Team play doesn't count for a thing." Scoop shrugged helplessly. "A lot of guys are impressed by that kind of talk."

"Besides," Matt pointed out, "Harsh's game is easier to play."

The three boys sat in thoughtful silence for several minutes. "Do you think there's anything we can do?" Win asked finally.

Matt looked at Win hopefully. "You've never

played against Dan Slade, have you? In scrimmage, I mean."

Win tried to think back. "No," he said at last. "I guess not."

"I think you're going to get your chance today."

"What makes you think so?"

Matt nodded emphatically. "Tom's nobody's fool. He knows what's going on." He tapped his massive fist against the palm of his hand to emphasize his points. "All modesty aside, Win. Who's Tom's first team?"

"I'll answer that," Scoop said promptly, ticking them off one by one. "Boots Lohman, Tony Parsons, Ed Walsh, Dan Slade, and our boy here."

"But what about Matt?" Win protested.

Matt shook his head. "We're being realistic now. Ed's better than I am. Sure, I know," he added. "Tom plans to use me a lot. But I'm sixth man in a five-man game." He brushed Win's objections aside with an easygoing grin. "I don't mind," he insisted. "Tom knows what's best for the team and I'd rather have it that way. But to get back to the point—Tom's starting five is being pulled apart by a couple of rotten apples. The way he's playing right now, Dan Slade's a liability and Ed Walsh isn't much better. For two weeks now, they've been sounding off about how they'd like a chance to play with some of their own kind. With some of the guys who go down to that Saturday morning class of Joe Harsh's." Matt leaned back with a grin of satisfaction. "I think Tom's going to give them a chance today."

Win stared at him curiously. "How do you know all this?" he asked. "Does Tom check with you these days?"

Matt laughed. "No, but Scoop here has been asked to report to practice this afternoon. Tom told him he was going to stage scrimmage just like a game. He wanted Scoop to keep time and score."

Win raised his eyebrows in surprise. "Tom's never done that before."

"He's desperate," Matt declared flatly. "Here it is Friday and our first game is next Wednesday night. Just four practice sessions away. He's got to make it clear to those guys that they're barking up the wrong tree when they play Harsh's style."

"How do you think he's going to manage that?"

"My guess is that he'll yank Dan Slade and Ed Walsh from the starting line-up and put in Charley Bantam and—I hope—me. He'll let them play their brand of ball. Our job will be to murder them."

Win whistled softly. "Sounds like kind of rough treatment."

"Yep," Matt agreed cheerfully. "Kill or cure. What do you say?"

"It's funny," Win said, getting up slowly. "On the first day of practice, Dan Slade told me to watch my step. He said I was a ball-hog."

"No kidding?" Scoop said wonderingly.

"That's right. He said team play was going to win us the championship." Win shook his head. "I wonder what got into him."

"Well, something has," Matt said. "But maybe we can straighten him out this afternoon."

"Maybe," Win said uncertainly. "I only hope it'll work."

"Amen," Scoop echoed. "Because we might as well face it. No matter what you think of Dan Slade, we need him if we're going to go all the way. He's a terrific ballplayer when he feels like it."

"Oh, he'll feel like playing today," Matt predicted grimly. "He'll want to show up Coach and the rest of us." He turned to Win solemnly. "That's your assignment, boy. Think you can stop him?"

Win felt the old competitive fire surge up as he smiled back at his two friends. "I don't know," he said. "But I'm going to give it a mighty big try."

CHAPTER SIX

The Exhibition

A GRIM-FACED Tom Joyce made the practice session short and perfunctory. And Win, now that his eyes had been opened by Matt and Scoop, could see that the coach was wasting his breath. Plays that should have been learned days ago were muffed or fell apart because Dan Slade or Ed Walsh or Red McGinley or any one of the three or four sophomores still on the Varsity simply didn't co-operate.

Wearily Tom kept calling them back and pointing out mistakes. But it didn't do any good. Finally, after about an hour of incredibly poor play, Tom blew his whistle.

"All right, boys," he called, "gather 'round." The players came shuffling over to Tom who was standing on the side lines by a scoring table that had been set up in front of the stands. "We're not getting anywhere," Tom declared tonelessly.

"Maybe you're working too hard. I don't know. But unless I see some better ball handling, we're going to have some changes around here. You fellows may not be aware of it, but our first game is only five days away. Now Framton's not in the Conference, so in a way it's a free game for us. Of course, I don't know about you, but I'd kind of like to win that one. It's always a good feeling to start out the season on top. So, here's what we're going to do. We'll split up into two teams and have a twenty-minute dress rehearsal. I'll referee and call fouls. Scoop Slocum will keep time and score. Divide up like this. Slade, Walsh, McGinley, Scholari and Jensen. Defending the south basket we'll have Lohman, Parsons, Hadley, Hughes and Bantam. Five-minute quarters. Slade and Lohman captain your two teams. We'll start in two minutes with a tap-up. Give me the buzzer when it's time, Scoop. The rest of you players," he said to the others, "can sit down and watch, maybe you'll learn something."

With that Tom walked off the court and stood silently to one side, apparently unmoved by the buzz of excitement that swept through the big gym. Everybody there knew what was going on, and, despite the fact that it was supposed to be only a scrimmage, Win felt an uneasy pull of tension mount up inside his body.

Working his shoulders back and forth to loosen his muscles, he trotted over to the huddle of ball-players under the south basket. As he took his place alongside Boots Lohman, Matt looked up and flashed him a grin.

"Just call me Madame La Zonga, the gypsy for-tuneteller," he growled happily. "I tell the future and read tea leaves, all for a very modest price."

"Go ahead," Boots Lohman replied. "Maybe you can tell us what's going to happen next?"

"Nothing easier," Matt assured him. "Give me your hand please," he said to Win. "Aha!" Matt cried, staring down at Win's palm. "I can see that in two minutes you will meet a fair-haired young man."

Charley Bantam smothered a grin. "What's his name?" he asked eagerly.

"Ssssh!" Matt cautioned. "It is coming clearer. What's this?" he cried in mock alarm. "The blond young man is not wearing trousers! Ahhh," he said with a relieved smile. "He has on short trousers. He is wearing basketball trunks—and a very swelled head."

"Yes, yes," Tony Parsons prompted. "What happens when they meet?"

"When they meet," Matt said gravely, "the blond young man will be murdered by our dark-haired young friend." He took a tighter grip on

Win's hand and spoke in his natural voice. "I really mean that, Win. Good luck."

"You bet," echoed Boots Lohman. "Fancy Dan needs somebody to take the wind out of his sails."

"So does that whole bunch," Tony Parsons muttered.

"Right," Boots nodded. "You fellows give me a signal when you want a time-out. In the meantime, we'll set up such a pace that it'll knock them off their feet. Okay?"

The others nodded and their hands met for the traditional pregame grip. Just as they broke from their huddle, Scoop sounded the warning horn and Win took his position downcourt from Boots. He had expected to be paired off with Red McGinley at the tap-up and was surprised to see Dan Slade waiting for him instead. Dan saw the questioning look on Win's face and answered it with a tight smile.

"How're you feeling, hot shot?" he asked unpleasantly.

"Pretty good," Win answered.

"I'm glad to hear it." Dan's smile disappeared and a grimly determined look took its place. "That way, there won't be any excuses." He ignored Win's outstretched hand and wheeled around to get set for the tap-up.

Win fought down a sudden flush of anger and

lined up beside him. Tom Joyce tossed up the ball and Boots Lohman had no trouble directing the tap toward Win. But just as he left his feet for the ball, Win felt a stinging blow against his ribs and a sharp blow against his hips that threw him off balance.

Dan had given him both elbow and hip on the first play, grabbed the ball, and was already over the mid-court line on his way to the basket.

Win recovered quickly and blasted off after Dan. Urging every last ounce of speed from his pumping legs, he slowly closed the gap. Win counted on Dan to try for the score himself and he wasn't disappointed. Just inside the free throw line, Dan went for the basket. With him came Win, a fraction of a second ahead of the ball, his hand reaching out for the lacing.

It was a clean save and Win managed to hang on to the ball as he landed on his feet. A quick look showed him that all of Dan's team had plunged recklessly after him, leaving Matt standing alone under his own basket. Win heaved a long, flat pass that bounced once. Matt took it a step away from the backboard and dropped it in.

"One for our side," Win thought to himself as he drifted over to cover Dan. The blond boy flashed him a hard look. "Lucky," he ground out. "It won't happen again."

"Why didn't you pass?" Win shot back. "You'd have made the point easy."

Dan flushed dangerously and turned away. Win took a step back and let Dan receive a pass. Then he shuffled in, covering Dan like a sheet. Dan dribbled over to his right, faked to his left and reversed. Win stuck to him like adhesive tape. Dan back-pedaled, charged and tried a double feint. Win gave him room for the maneuver, but blocked all forward motion. Dan put on a sudden burst of speed and tried a wide sweep around to the left. At the side lines, he put on the brakes and tried to barrel in toward his basket. Win was waiting for him. Dan moved back, his eyes restlessly searching for an opening. But Win refused to be sucked in and kept on his toes, waiting for Dan to commit himself.

By now the other players had stopped all motion. It had become a personal duel between Dan and Win, and they knew it. Win was unaware that the big gym was silent except for the steady *tap-tap* of Dan's dribbling. He was watching the anger mount in Dan's face and knew that in his furious determination to break through, Dan was probably going to make a mistake.

It came sooner than he had expected. Seeing that he was still unable to shake off his unruffled guard, Dan angrily bounced the ball too hard. It came up a little faster than he had anticipated and for a moment he fumbled. That was all the time Win needed. His long arm darted out, flicked it away from Dan's groping fingers and drove for the basket. Dan was caught flat-footed as he watched Win sink an easy lay-up shot.

The whistle blew and Win hurried back to pick up Dan. He saw Red McGinley rifle a short pass to Teddy Scholari. Teddy tried to take it down, but Matt was all over him and he handed off to Jensen. Jensen looked downcourt for a free receiver, but couldn't find one. Charley Bantam was beginning to crowd him and he knew he had to get it off soon and yelled for a taker.

Out of the corner of his eye, Win saw Dan make a gesture of impatience as he moved around to get Jensen out of his box. Win trailed along, playing Dan purposefully loose. But as Jensen thankfully heaved a slow, soft lob over to Dan, Win exploded into action. His interception practically took the ball right out of Dan's waiting hands. Without breaking stride, Win swooped down toward his basket, and as he heard Dan breathing hard behind him, jammed to a stop and drew to one side.

Dan's figure came flying wildly past him in a last-minute attempt to change direction, but it was too late. Win heard Dan land with a bone-jarring thump beyond the out-of-play line as he poured in an easy bank shot to make it 6-0 for his team.

After the whistle, Scholari took the ball for a second time and again was stopped by Matt. Moving before he was ready, he tried to heave it to Jensen, but Matt blocked it. The two boys dived after the ball and grabbed it at the same time. Tom Joyce's whistle called it a held ball and the two teams lined up for the jump.

Win was pretty sure Dan would try another foul on the jump, and this time he was ready for it. As Tom tossed up the ball, Win held back for a fraction of a second and so was able to avoid Dan's elbow. Dan realized he had been tricked and whirled around to find Win and the ball. Just as he did so, Win leaped forward to snare the tap which Matt had won easily and felt Dan's foot trip over his outstretched leg. Dan catapulted through the air and skidded awkwardly on his side. Win ignored him and shot a high pass to Boots. The big center moved gracefully into the keyhole as Win broke for the corner. Matt cut around behind Boots who set up a screen for the rugged guard as he lunged for the basket, faked a jump shot and handed off to Charley Bantam. Charley zigzagged downcourt, then rifled a fast one to Tony Parsons. Tony went around his guard as if he had been carved out of a block of wood and, as the defense converged on him, went up for what looked like a sure shot, drawing two of the other team with him. But instead of going for the basket, he threw a beautiful underhand pass to Win in the corner. Win took it chest-high, faked, drew a foul from Red McGinley and went up for the score. His free throw rippled through the cords to tally his seventh point in less than four minutes.

By the end of the first five-minute quarter, Win's team was ahead by the lopsided score of 17-2. Win had sunk two more—a beautiful set shot from mid-court and a hook shot from the side. In addition, Boots Lohman and Tony had both found the range for a tally apiece.

At the end of the half, with the score standing at 42-8, Tom Joyce called a halt. "There's no point in going on with this," he said scornfully. "You fellows," he said, turning to Dan and his friends, "you fellows can't even make change. I don't know where you learned that kind of basketball—I know it wasn't from me. But wherever it was, you'd better forget it. The way you're playing now, you couldn't make the junior varsity of a girls' school team." Dan and the others stared sullenly down at the court, refusing to look Tom in the eye.

"All right," Tom finished angrily. "That's all for today. I want you back here Monday afternoon at three-thirty, and I want you to be ready to play basketball." He paused and looked around significantly. "My kind of basketball. Are there any questions?"

When nobody said a word, Tom turned and stalked off the court, leaving behind him a subdued and considerably chastened squad of basketball players.

CHAPTER SEVEN

A Vicious Attack

ON SATURDAYS, Win usually slept until eight-thirty or nine, but on the day following the scrimmage, he was wide awake by seven-thirty. Knowing he had another hour and a half in bed if he wanted it, he bunched the covers irritably around his head and determined to get some sleep. But it was hopeless.

Win had gone directly home after practice the day before. Usually he stopped along the way to meet the gang at the Malt Shop, but for some reason that afternoon he didn't want to talk about what had happened. He needed some time alone to think things over for himself.

He spent the evening reading—or trying to read, answering his mother's questions so mechanically that she finally asked him what was the matter. The trouble was, he couldn't tell her. He didn't know himself. About one thing, however, he was certain. He didn't particularly enjoy humiliating his team-mates. He only hoped it did some good.

He wished he could talk to Walt, but his brother had gone out early for a meeting of the Chamber of Commerce and wasn't expected back until late. Finally, at about ten-thirty, he said good night to his mother and went upstairs.

The night's sleep accomplished one thing, at least. It made him want to talk to someone, to com-pare notes and get another opinion about the scrimmage. He decided to walk over to Matt's house directly after breakfast.

But Matt must have had the same thought, ex-cept that his came a little earlier. Win was just about to sit down to a stack of pancakes and bacon when his pal peered in from the back porch.

"Mind if I come in?" Matt said, rapping politely on the already half-open door.

"Matt!" Mrs. Hadley exclaimed. "Of course you can. You're up early this morning."

"Yes'm," Matt agreed, shouldering his way into the kitchen.

"Had your breakfast yet?"

"Oh yes," Matt assured her, but his eyes shone when he saw Win's plate dripping with melted butter and clear maple syrup.

"Sit down," Mrs. Hadley laughed. "The pan's still greased and hot."

Matt shot her a grateful glance and eased himself down beside Win. "It was a long walk over," Matt explained apologetically. "Kinda sharpened my appetite a little."

Mrs. Hadley poured some creamy batter into the pan and smiled. "I didn't know it ever needed any sharpening, Matt. I thought it was always like a razor."

"Well," Matt admitted, "I don't have too much trouble in that direction."

"So I've noticed," Mrs. Hadley observed dryly. "What brought you over this morning?"

Matt dug in his back pocket and dragged out a well-thumbed copy of the *Crawford Record*. Win saw that it was folded back to the Dixboro page. "Seen the paper this morning?" Matt asked.

Mrs. Hadley shook her head. "No, we're getting it late this week. Little Petey Jackson, our regular delivery boy, is sick. The fellow on the next route brings it to us after he's through with his regular customers."

"Well, take a look at this!" Matt laid the paper down on the table.

"Read it to us, Win," his mother said.

Win propped up the paper and began:

FIREWORKS LIGHT UP PRACTICE AS
SEASON OPENER FOUR DAYS OFF

With Dixboro launching its hoop season next Wednesday night, four short days off, Cougar coach Tom Joyce has apparently dropped all drills in favor of a personal grudge match with Joe Harsh, mentor of the newly formed Dixboro Midgets.

This last-mentioned team, you may remember, was organized by a number of prominent Dixboro citizens in order to raise the standard of local basketball on the sound theory that says, "If you want to train them right, start 'em young."

No one in town quarrels with this theory—except Tom Joyce, who has had his way with Dixboro athletics for so long that he is beginning to believe he has a personal patent on anybody who picks up a ball or tries on a uniform.

The bitter private feud between the two coaches stems from what should merely have been a difference of opinion. Tom Joyce teaches one kind of basketball; Joe Harsh, another. This department believes in giving both systems a chance. Harsh isn't treading on Tom Joyce's toes by teaching a few eighth-graders how to throw a ball into a basket.

He does this, incidentally, on Saturday mornings—the only time he has the use of the elementary school gym. These informal get-togethers are well attended, not only by the Midgets, of course, but by some members of the Varsity Squad. And there's the rub.

When some of the Varsity players tried to improve their own game by adopting some of Harsh's tips, Coach Tom Joyce blew up.

He refused to consider their ideas and insisted they play his way. The result of Joyce's inflexible attitude has been to create serious friction within Varsity ranks.

This friction exploded into open warfare yesterday during a scrimmage held at Alumni Gym. In a twenty-minute exhibition game that went only half the scheduled time, Joyce pitted the rebels on his squad against the boys he knew he could count on. The old reliables, spearheaded by some flashy playing by Win Hadley, beat the opposition, captained by that fine player, Dan Slade.

Come, come, Tom. That was no test and you know it. Slade's team was confused and uncertain.

Three weeks ago, this department predicted that Dixboro would take the championship. But now, in the cold light of Friday's sorry spectacle, we are reluctantly forced to change our minds. Tom Joyce may still pull a rabbit out of the hat on Wednesday night. But this department doubts it. Unless the Cougar coach steps down from his platform of outraged dignity and stops playing off some boys against others, Framton will walk all over us.

On second thought, here's a suggestion. Why not let Joe Harsh's Midgets play Framton's Varsity? They'll probably make a better showing. At least they're a team with spirit that's going places.

And speaking of going places, one place they're headed is the elementary school gym for more frequent practice. The issue comes up before the Board of Education this evening at eight o'clock. Everyone interested in broadening Dixboro's athletic horizons should make a point of attending. It's an open meeting.

In this department's first article some weeks ago on the Varsity's hoop chances for the coming season, the column ended with the words, ". . . Here's to Coach Tom Joyce and the Cougars."

Today's column will sign off with this message: "Here's to Coach Joe Harsh and the Midgets."

Win put the paper back on the table with a shaking hand. He looked at Matt and tried to speak. "I . . . I . . ."

Matt nodded. "Yeah," he said. "I know."

"But what's come over the man?"

Matt shrugged. "Search me."

"I've never read such a vicious article in all my

life. It's full of distortions and half-truths. He twists everything around and—"

"Take it easy, Win," Matt counseled quietly.

Win jumped up from the table and began to pace back and forth angrily. "Does he think that kind of talk will *help* the team?"

"I don't know."

As the boys were talking excitedly, Mrs. Hadley drifted over to the table and took a closer look at the column. "It's funny," she said with a slight frown. "Walt said there'd be something like this in the paper this morning."

Win stopped and stared at his mother. "How did he know?"

Mrs. Hadley shook her head. "I don't know. He came in last night after you went to bed, Win. He seemed pretty upset about something. I guess something that happened at the Chamber of Commerce meeting. He said Neal Travers was there with some other men, laughing about the article on Tom Joyce."

Win started out of the kitchen with sudden decision. "I'm going down to the showroom and talk to Walt right now," he said.

"He's not there," Mrs. Hadley said. "He's gone over to Crawford to look at some used cars the firm might buy. He won't be back until late this afternoon."

Win stopped and walked slowly back into the kitchen. "There's something fishy going on," he said thoughtfully. "Neal Travers wouldn't write such an article all by himself. Somebody must have talked him into it."

"But why?" Matt asked.

"I wouldn't know." He stopped beside Matt's chair and grinned unexpectedly. "What do you say the two of us take a little walk?"

"Where?"

"Over to the elementary school gym. I'd like to see this great new team in action. We probably won't get much information, but I think it's a good idea if we know a little more about Joe Harsh and his wonderful brand of basketball."

Matt polished off a last mountainous forkful of pancakes and gulped in agreement. "All right," he said, draining his milk. "Let's get educated."

CHAPTER EIGHT

Tommy Burton

IT WAS barely nine o'clock by the time Win and Matt walked into the elementary school gym, but the floor was already crowded with action. About a dozen husky youngsters were heaving the ball back and forth with pep and determination.

"Hey," Win said wonderingly. "Maybe Joe Harsh isn't doing such a bad job after all."

Excited cries and an occasional cheer for a good shot came from all over the court as the boys fought doggedly for the ball and then drove for the basket.

"Take a look at that," Matt laughed, pointing to a sawed-off runt of a boy whose sneakers were practically falling off his feet. The boy was gripping the ball close to his chest and was winding up for a desperate heave at the basket more than thirty feet away. "I bet he won't even reach the backboard," Matt predicted.

Matt was right. The ball fell several feet short into an eager huddle of players. There was a ragged yell as a half-dozen pairs of arms scrambled wildly. Then suddenly, out of the confusion, a lithe youngster made a perfectly timed leap, grabbed the ball and landed easily on his feet. Three or four players converged on him immediately, but the youngster faked one of them out of position, pivoted neatly around another, and cut through the hole between his two remaining opponents. Win and Matt both gasped in astonishment. It was done with the aplomb and grace of a veteran. But at the very last, the boy made a mistake. He kept on going for the basket.

"Reverse!" Win thought to himself. "Reverse!" He almost shouted it out in his eagerness to help.

But the ball carrier charged ahead. When he saw he was boxed in, he dropped one shoulder and slammed against one of his guards, sending him to the floor. The guard bounced back to his feet with an indignant yell. "Foul!" he cried hotly. "That was a foul!"

The youngster with the ball stopped and glared back. "It was not!" he insisted. "You were in the way!"

"But you can't charge a guy like that!"

"Who says?"

"The rule book says!"

"Aaah," came the disgusted answer.

The argument probably would have continued if one of the players hadn't spotted Win and Matt standing quietly along the side lines. "Hey look, fellahs!" he shouted. "Look who's here!"

The rhubarb on the floor died down as the two teams stared over at Win and Matt with obvious respect. "Gee!" someone whispered. "That's Win Hadley!"

"Yeah," came the awed reply. "And that's Matt Hughes with him."

"Let's ask them," a voice piped up.

"Good idea," came a chorus. "They'll know."

The boy who had been dribbling the ball was pushed forward to do the asking. He walked up to Win and Matt haltingly. "Hi," he said shyly.

"Hi."

"Listen, did you two fellows see that last play?"

"We sure did," Win nodded. "You did a nice job." The boy's face flushed with pleasure. "Up to the end," Win added. "You should have reversed instead of trying to crash through."

The boy's face fell. "Yeah," he mumbled. "I guess so. But what I really wanted to know, was there a foul on the play?"

Both boys nodded emphatically. "There sure was," Matt replied.

"Well, who did it?"

"You did."

The younger boy accepted the judgment and nodded. "Charging, huh?"

"Right," Matt said.

"Okay, thanks." He turned to his fellow players. "You win," he cried. He tossed the basketball back out on the court. "Your ball."

Before he could follow it, Win reached out and grabbed him by the arm. "Wait a minute," he said. "What's your name?"

"Tommy," the boy replied. "Tommy Burton."

"Eighth grade?" Tommy nodded. "Friend of Freddie Slade?"

Tommy made a sour face and shook his head. "That drip!" was his comment.

Win grinned down at the boy. "Well, forget about him. I just wanted to tell you that you're pretty good. You're going to make quite a basketball player. Does Tom Joyce know about you?"

Tommy shrugged indifferently. "Who knows?" He tried to act as if it didn't matter, but the pose didn't last long. "Hey, you really think so?" he said eagerly.

"Sure. I wouldn't say it if I didn't mean it."

Tommy turned on a happy grin and then turned

it off as he was suddenly struck by an idea. "Listen," he said, "you fellows wouldn't like to . . . I mean if you don't have anything better to do, maybe you wouldn't mind refereeing the game?" He jerked a grimy thumb out at the floor.

Win smiled at him but shook his head. "I'm afraid we can't." He pointed to his feet. "No sneakers."

Tommy understood, but he looked so disappointed that Win felt he ought to say something. "I'll tell you what I'll do, though," he added. "I'll come by next Saturday and referee. So will Matt, if we can make it."

"I can make it!" Matt said heartily.

Tommy's eyes lit up like a Christmas tree. He darted out on the court, changed his mind and ran back. "Thanks," he said earnestly. "You don't know what that'll . . . Wow! I'll see you here next Saturday around seven-thirty. Okay?"

Win gulped. "Seven-thirty!" He could feel Matt wince at the prospect. "Why so early?"

"That's when the janitor gets here to open up," Tommy explained simply, "and he kinda keeps an eye on us and lets us play."

Win looked at the boys in amazement. "You mean you've been playing here since seven-thirty?"

Tommy nodded. "We gotta," he said. "They take the court away from us at nine-thirty."

"Who does?"

"Freddie Slade. And Mr. Harsh."

It suddenly dawned on Win that the boys they had been watching weren't the Midgets. This was a pickup team that played for fun because they loved the game. "How about playing in the afternoon?" Win suggested.

Tommy ruled that out. "Can't. Some of the guys have jobs. They gotta help out at home."

Win didn't say anything to that. He found himself staring down at the court. "We used to play here all morning long," Tommy was saying. "But that's out now."

"Yeah," Win said grimly. "That's out now. You fellows like to play?"

Tommy's eyes lit up again. "Boy!" he breathed. "Do we!"

"What about joining Freddie Slade's team?"

Tommy gave a short, hard laugh. "We tried."

"What happened?"

"He told us to scram. He said it was his team."

"What did Mr. Harsh say?"

"He backed up Freddie."

In the silence that followed, a plaintive voice cried out from the court. "Hey, come on, Tommy! Let's go! It's getting late."

Tommy turned with an impatient gesture. "Go on without me," he ordered. "I'm busy." A general razzberry greeted this remark, but the boys went back to their game.

Matt smiled at him. "You must be the boss of the gang," he observed.

Tommy's reaction was entirely unexpected. He turned on Matt with a look of fury. "It's not a gang!" he shouted angrily. For a second, Win thought the little fellow was going to throw himself at Matt, but then the awkward moment passed. Matt put an apologetic hand on Tommy's shoulder. "Look," he said slowly. "I don't know what I said wrong. But I'm sorry. Okay?"

Tommy scuffed his sneaker moodily along the floor. "That's what Mr. Harsh called us," he muttered. "He said we weren't anything better than a street gang." He looked up at them seriously. "But we're not," he said. "All we want to do is play basketball."

For the second time in the conversation, Win didn't know quite what to say. Instead, he nodded understandingly. "Sure," he said at last. "There must be a way."

Tommy's black look vanished. "You think so?" he said eagerly.

"I don't know of any," Win admitted. "But I'll ask around. Maybe Tom Joyce will have an idea."

"You'd do that for us?" Tommy asked breathlessly.

"Sure," Win said. "I can't promise anything, though."

Tommy stuck out his hand. "That's a deal. I'll see you later."

But before he could return to the game, the doors to the downstairs locker room flew open and a second group of boys came into the gym. Most of them were taller than Tommy and his pals and all sported brand-new uniforms with DIXBORO MIDGETS emblazoned over their fronts. At their head came Freddie Slade and Joe Harsh.

When Harsh saw Tommy still on the floor, he blew his whistle angrily. "All right, you!" he cried in his unpleasantly nasal voice. "Clear out!"

Win saw Tommy's face harden, but he beckoned to his friends. Dejectedly they trudged off the court in the other direction.

"Not even allowed to use the locker room," Matt growled. "I bet they have to dress in a classroom somewhere."

Win nodded, but his eyes were on Freddie Slade. Dan's younger brother was watching Tommy's departure with a crooked smile of triumph. Standing beside him, Joe Harsh looked cold and unrelenting until he suddenly caught sight of Win and Matt.

"Well, well," he cried in greeting. "We've got some newcomers this morning. I thought you boys would be around."

"Just curious," Win said mildly. "Mind if we watch?"

"Not at all," Harsh said jovially. "You can take notes if you want to. Maybe Tom Joyce would like to see some of them."

Win heard a rumble of anger from Matt and he put a restraining hand on the big fellow's arm. "Maybe he would, Mr. Harsh."

"On the other hand," Harsh added after a pause, "I think he's probably read enough today. It wouldn't do to strain his eyes." Harsh was obviously referring to Neal Travers' article in the *Record*.

Win steadfastly refused to rise to the bait. "Tom Joyce has got pretty good eyesight," Win replied calmly. "He can usually read most anything—even what's between the lines."

For some reason, Win's shot struck home. Harsh flushed angrily and then abruptly turned his back. "All right, Midgets!" he shouted. "We'll have a warm-up drill."

Win and Matt moved back out of the way and settled down to watch. It was one of the most amazing exhibitions of basketball they had ever seen. Every boy on the squad went out of his way to make sure that Freddie got all the shots.

Passing was limited and there was hardly any

playmaking, although Win had to admit that the boys had plenty of drive. Whenever Freddie had the ball, he drove in to try for the score. Several times he fouled his opponents, but Harsh never once blew the whistle.

Finally, on one play, Freddie hit his guard a twisting shoulder blow that sent him falling on his face. The boy got to his feet, shaking his head and doing his best to fight back his tears.

Harsh blasted away on his whistle. "What's the matter with you?" he cried angrily. "Can't you take it?"

The boy looked down at his shoes.

"So what, if he roughed you up?" Harsh demanded. "Rough him back. You boys have got to be tougher. Give as good as you get and keep driving. All right now, let's see you all show some of Freddie's spirit."

Win could hardly believe his ears. "Let's get out of here," he said to Matt. "I've seen enough."

Matt nodded angrily, "So that's the kind of basketball Harsh teaches them!" He shook his head in disgust and reached for the door. "If that's called 'broadening Dixboro's athletic horizons,' I'll take mine nice and narrow."

"Right," Win agreed as they went through the door.

"Hey!" came a voice from a nearby staircase. "You won't forget, huh?" It was Tommy Burton, dressed and ready to leave.

"Don't worry," Win assured him. "I'll talk to Tom Joyce today."

"Great. I'll be seeing you." Tommy gave them a nod and disappeared.

"Well, well," drawled another, more familiar, voice behind them. "You fellows sure have strange taste in friends." It was Dan Slade, lounging carelessly against the gym door. In his hand, Win noticed, he was carrying a copy of the *Crawford Record*. It was open at Neal Travers' column.

"Hello, Dan," Win replied. "You mean little Tommy Burton?"

"Yeah, I mean him."

"He's going to end up being a good ballplayer," Win answered. "We were just watching him."

"Keep right on watching him," Dan said. "Don't ever take your eyes off him. But he's not going to end up where you think."

"No?"

"No. He's going to end up in reform school if he doesn't watch his step. Ask your buddy, Tom Joyce. He knows." Dan chuckled meaningfully and pushed his way into the gym, leaving Win and Matt to stare after him in open-mouthed astonishment.

CHAPTER NINE

A Private Conversation

IT MIGHT BE said of Tom Joyce that you couldn't really appreciate him until you had been out of school for a couple of years. He had a reputation as a strict disciplinarian. A few even called him cold. But once a boy got away from Tom Joyce and had a chance to compare his values with the values of the outside world, he suddenly realized that Tom Joyce was not only a great coach. He was a great teacher and a great man.

His loyalty to Dixboro and the boys who had played under him was legendary. On every block in Dixboro there were young men who had been helped by Tom's generosity. He had found jobs for some. Some he had urged to go to college, helping them with their efforts to pay their own way if money was scarce. Tom had probably attended more weddings and stood as godfather at more christenings than any other man in town. That was just one of the lesser known but pleasanter chores that went along with being head coach and athletic director of a small-town high school.

In his college days, Tom had toyed with the idea of becoming a professional. He was twice named to the All-American team as a quarterback, posted a three-year batting average of .477 in baseball, and was voted the most valuable basketball player of the National Invitation Tournament in his senior year. Three different ball clubs wanted to sign him for their Triple-A farm system, while a professional football team asked him to join spring training.

After a lot of deep thinking, Tom turned them all down in favor of a job as assistant coach at a small New England high school nobody had ever heard of.

"What in the world does he want to go to Dixboro for?" his amazed friends asked each other. "He'll bury himself up there."

Tom hadn't thought so twenty years ago, and he didn't think so now. He had arrived in Dixboro with a firm resolve that the years never dimmed. Time changed Tom Joyce. It turned his close-cropped brown hair to an iron-gray. It etched deep lines in his darkly tanned face. But time never changed his mind about Dixboro and his job. "The best job in the world," he always said to anyone who asked. "Coaching boys is an experience few men are lucky enough to have. I'm grateful I've had the chance."

Tom was sincere in his feelings. He felt an almost personal sense of involvement in the triumphs and failures, the problems of his boys. And he knew enough to keep his mouth closed. That was one reason why Tom Joyce had the reputation of being a good man to talk to. And that was why Win Hadley found himself on the steps of Alumni Gym a little before eleven that morning, after a fruitless visit to Tom's house. Matt had left him a few minutes earlier because of an errand he had promised to run for his father. But before they parted, they agreed to get together again later that afternoon.

At first Win thought the big gymnasium building was deserted. But as he made his way down the long corridor behind the locker rooms, he knew Tom Joyce was in his office. He could tell by the sharp odor of tobacco smoke that drifted down the hall.

Tom was careful about his smoking because he believed in setting a good example for his boys. But on a quiet Saturday morning, in the privacy of his office, he sometimes relaxed his rule. Coaching was a lonely job. There were often difficult decisions for him to make, and an occasional pipe helped him think through his problems.

A hearty "Come in!" answered Win's knock. Tom seemed delighted but surprised to see him.

"Sit down, Win," he said pleasantly, leaning forward to brush a pile of papers from the room's other chair. Win saw a copy of the *Crawford Record* disappear under a sheaf of scouting reports, so he knew that Tom had read the article. "What can I do for you?" Tom was saying.

Win sat forward uncomfortably and tried to make a beginning. "I . . . I read Neal Travers' column this morning," he started.

Tom smiled ruefully. "So did everybody else in town," he said. "The phone never stopped ringing at home, so I came here to get some peace."

"I'm sorry about it, Coach," Win said sincerely.

Tom brushed it aside. "It's happened before," he said. "It'll happen again. You get used to it."

"But it was never quite as bad as this," Win protested.

"No," Tom admitted. "He did pile it on and that's a fact."

"What about the people who called you?" Win asked eagerly. "Did they back you up?"

Tom leaned back and drew easily on his pipe. "They all wanted to know what was going on. Most of them demanded to know if it was true. Some of them were pretty angry. But some—" he paused and smiled warmly—"some of them said they'd stand by me. It's nice to have friends." He sat up and drew his chair closer to Win's. "But that's not what you came to see me about, is it?"

"Well, it's part of it," Win said. "You see, Matt Hughes and I went over to the elementary school gym this morning to get a look at Harsh and the Midgets."

"And?"

Win shrugged. "It was hard to watch. They're being taught the worst kind of basketball."

Tom nodded silently. "I know," he said finally. "But nobody will believe it."

"They will if they ever see them play," Win declared.

Surprisingly, Tom shook his head. "I think they could beat every other elementary school team around," he said flatly.

"But you've always said that it's not winning that matters in the end. It's how you play the game," Win said, in some surprise.

"Oh yes," Tom said. "I feel like that; I hope most of my boys do. But I'm afraid many people are just interested in seeing a winning team, and they're not too particular about how it's done."

"You really think the Midgets are that good?"

"They're natural athletes, a lot of them," Tom explained. "Freddie Slade, in particular, is going to be a first-class player. They have it all over the other elementary school teams in the area because —we might as well face it—*none* of them have been coached too well. I know," he added, "because I've seen them."

He smiled at Win's surprised expression. "You didn't know I scouted the elementary school teams? Well, sure I do. I like to know what's coming up in the way of talent." He sighed and shook his head. "Believe me, Win. Freddie Slade and his Midgets can take 'em all. I don't care how they've been coached."

"I know a team they couldn't take," Win replied.

Tom put aside his pipe and looked at Win with interest. "Who?"

"Ever hear of a kid called Tommy Burton?"

Tom chuckled and threw one leg over the side of his chair. "Isn't that funny?" he said. "I knew you were going to mention his name."

"Well, I saw him play today, and he's good."

"I know he is."

"And there are a couple of other fellows in that bunch of his. Gee, I think they could give the Midgets a real run for their money."

Tom stared thoughtfully out the window. "Maybe you're right, but who's going to coach them? Where are they going to practice?" He looked sharply back at Win. "I suppose you know they try to squeeze in a couple of hours every Saturday morning before Harsh chases them off the court? That's not enough time to build a team."

Win shook his head in admiration. "How did you know about that? I just found out this morning."

Tom passed it off with a shrug and reached for his pipe again. "Any suggestions?"

"Not at the moment," Win admitted. He thought for a moment about his next question, then decided to ask it bluntly. "Is Tommy Burton in trouble?"

Tom's match was suspended over the bowl of his pipe for a fraction of a second. He threw Win a shrewd glance and proceeded to light up. "That depends," he said between puffs, "on what you call trouble."

"Dan Slade said he was headed for reform school."

Tom grunted and snuffed out his match. "I'd say that was a slight case of exaggeration. Tommy's a difficult kid and he's been in hot water more than once." Tom paused and seemed undecided about something. Finally he hitched himself back into an upright position and spoke very quietly.

"What I'm going to tell you now will never leave this room. Okay?"

Win nodded.

"All right. A year ago Tommy was caught stealing money from a school locker. Naturally he was brought up before the principal for questioning. Police don't usually get called into cases like that.

But this one was an exception. He just happened to pick on Freddie Slade's locker."

Win whistled softly.

"Freddie was good and mad and told his father. That brought Mr. Slade roaring into the principal's office like a tornado. He said he wanted Tommy hauled before Juvenile Court and put away. It was all they could do to calm him down long enough to listen to the whole story. Tommy admitted the theft. There was never any question about that. But—and here was the bombshell—Tommy claimed he had a right to the money. He said it belonged to him."

"That sounds strange. Why didn't he ask for it?"

"He did. Several times. But Freddie refused to turn it over. The money, you see, was part of a bet Tommy won from Freddie. It was during the World Series between the Yankees and the Braves, remember?"

"Sure," Win said. "The Braves were out in front and the Yankees took it in the last game."

"That's it. Tommy Burton's a Yankee fan and he insisted that they'd win the Series, even when it looked bad for them. Freddie heard him and made him a bet.

"How much did they bet?"

"Two dollars. It was all the money Tommy could afford and quite a sum for him. Well, anyway, after the Yankees won, Tommy kept asking Freddie for the money. Freddie kept teasing him and laughing at him, and that went on through the end of November. Finally Tommy got mad. His mother's birthday was coming up and he wanted to buy her something nice. He went up to Freddie for the last time and Freddie told him he'd never give it to him. If he wanted it, he'd have to come and get it. So Tommy did."

"What did Mr. Slade say to that?"

"First he said it was a lie. His son would never do a thing like that. Tommy insisted it was the truth and said he had witnesses."

"And did he?"

"Yes. The witnesses were brought into the principal's office one by one. They all swore up and down that they had heard Tommy and Freddie make the bet."

"I guess that finished Mr. Slade," Win said.

"Not quite," Tom said grimly. "He switched his argument and said it was obvious that Freddie was just fooling around and teasing—and would have paid up eventually. And, of course, there was the fact you couldn't get around—Tommy *had* taken the money from Freddie's locker."

"What happened then?"

"Nothing very much. The principal got Mr. Slade to agree not to press charges and he marched off with his son. The whole affair was hushed up."

"How did you get involved in it?"

"Me?" Tom settled back in his chair with a smile. "The principal thought it might be a good idea if I had a talk with Tommy. So I went around to his house and saw the whole family. We must have talked half the night. I think Tommy saw where he was wrong—no, I'll take that back. I *know* he saw. He was pretty ashamed of himself, even if he did have some justification. He's a good kid," Tom said fondly. "He didn't whine or cry to get out of it. And then when he saw he was wrong, he was willing to admit it. No, I don't think Tommy's going to get into much trouble in the future. I don't even think he's going to do much betting on athletic events. He's learned his lesson. It was a mistake and that's that. The story is closed."

"Dan Slade didn't seem to think so," Win said softly.

"I'm afraid they still don't trust Tommy. There's a lot of ill will there."

"So that's why Tommy was never allowed to play on the Midgets," Win mused. He looked up at Tom angrily. "I think it's a dirty shame," he said suddenly.

"Really?" There was a searching look on Tom's face as he glanced at Win. "Do you feel strongly enough about it to do something?"

Win nodded vehemently. "You bet I do!"

"Even if it means taking up a lot of your spare time?"

"I don't care," Win said firmly. "It's unfair to have a restricted team in this town." He returned Tom's look with equal seriousness. "I mean that," he said. "It's important enough to fight for."

Tom nodded approvingly. "You know there's a meeting of the School Board tonight? And I guess you know what it's about. Can you be there?"

"Me? Sure."

"All right then. I want you to back me up on something I'm going to say at that meeting."

"But why me? I can't do anything?"

"Oh, yes, you can. When it comes right down to it, you're the only one who can."

"I still don't understand why?"

"Because you want to," Tom said simply. "Because you think it's important."

"Well, sure, but . . ."

"Don't interrupt. I want to put a proposition to you and I want your frank answer. What you say now will determine what I say tonight, and may decide whether or not Tommy Burton and his friends get a place to practice. Are you game?"

Win nodded, and Tom pulled his chair up beside him and began talking in a quiet, urgent voice.

CHAPTER TEN

Win Gets a Job

LARGELY BECAUSE OF Neal Travers' article in the *Crawford Record*, the School Board meeting that night was heavily attended. It was hard to judge how many of the audience were there because they were seriously concerned about the issues, and how many had come along just to see the fireworks. In any event, the auditorium was practically full by the time Win arrived shortly before eight, and he was forced to find a seat in the rear.

Dr. Chalmers, the Superintendent, opened the meeting by expressing his pleasure at seeing so many people there. He spoke of how happy he was to see a growing awareness among the citizens of Dixboro of the educational problems facing the Board.

After a few more polite generalities, he explained that this was a meeting called for a special purpose and recognized Mr. Slade as the first speaker. Dan's father, looking like a wrestler about to enter the ring, advanced toward the center of the platform, bowed slightly and began to speak.

"For some time now," he said, "your School Board has been concerned with the recreational facilities of the elementary school. Spring and fall present no problems. The children have adequate outdoor playing areas. However, in the winter, the entire school is thrown upon the resources of one gymnasium. I need hardly point out that this is a most unsatisfactory arrangement. The answer is obvious. A new and larger gymnasium must be built. What we are proposing to do tonight is to take the first step toward that goal."

There was an excited buzz of conversation around the auditorium as the full meaning of Mr. Slade's words sank in. Very clever, Win thought to himself. It was a good beginning for the other side.

Dan's father held up his hand for silence. "As you all know, building a new gymnasium is an expensive undertaking. The money must come from somewhere. Unfortunately, having recently constructed the new high school gym, the School Board will be severely limited in borrowing power for several years to come. I needn't go into all the technicalities except to say that we can't start anything new until we've paid our old debts. I think

that makes sense to everyone here. However—"
and here Mr. Slade raised a hopeful finger—
"financing a new building is a distinct possibility if
we can attract fresh capital. By that I mean new
businesses, new people coming in to settle in Dixboro. They would, by their very presence, increase
available funds because they would contribute sub-
stantially to the tax revenues. This, in turn, would
give us more money to spend and would, almost
certainly, make the new elementary gym a reality."

On all sides, Win could feel people nodding
their approval. He leaned forward to concentrate
on Mr. Slade's argument.

"The matter of attracting new capital to Dixboro," he was saying, "is the prime concern of our
Chamber of Commerce, headed so ably by Mr.
George Ross. Working together, the Chamber of
Commerce and the School Board have explored a
number of ideas. Our first problem was to find an
effective means of getting people to know that
Dixboro is on the map. I suppose we could adver-
tise by telling people to come to Dixboro—it's a
nice place to live and so forth—but that's expensive and maybe they wouldn't believe us."

A ripple of laughter shimmered through the
auditorium and Mr. Slade acknowledged it with
a tight smile.

"Fortunately," he went on, "we have a splendid

example of how a nearby community has managed to sell itself to outside interests. I am referring, of course, to Crawford, with a population that is larger than ours and with a business center that is growing all the time. How did Crawford do it? People from all over the state have heard of Crawford. Why?"

Mr. Slade paused dramatically and the audience waited eagerly to hear his answer.

"Well, there are a number of reasons, but certainly one of the biggest is that Crawford consistently has winning teams in every sport. People like sports and they like winners. I don't care if it's football, basketball or baseball, Crawford nearly always sends out teams that go to the top or near the top of the Conference. Because of that, they get state-wide publicity. Everyone has heard of Crawford. Now we know perfectly well that Crawford didn't get where it is by accident, and it's not because they're a bunch of supermen, either." Again there was a ripple of laughter.

"They did it because they planned well and started training their boys early. In the seventh and eighth grades, Crawford boys have a chance to learn the fundamentals of team sports. Now maybe you see how all this ties together. There's no reason in the world why we can't do the same thing, and that's exactly what we're proposing to do. On a smaller scale, of course," he added hastily. "We've found a man who's willing to coach an elementary school team. Some of you may know him. His name is Joe Harsh. Frankly, we'd like to give him a chance to see what he can do. At first, the team would be strictly unofficial. We'd try to schedule a few informal games with some of the other elementary school teams. If our boys do well, then next year we can consider hiring a regular coach and entering them into organized competition. All in all, I think you'll have to admit that it sounds like a pretty good idea."

The audience seemed to think so because people all around Win nodded their heads.

"The only drawback to the whole plan," Mr. Slade continued, "is the problem of finding practice space." He spoke more slowly now, choosing his words with great care. "But if you look at it one way, there really isn't much of a problem. As it's being used now, the elementary school gym doesn't do anybody much good. It's just too crowded. Now what we propose to do," he went on in a more confident voice, "is to turn that gym over to a group that can make the best use of it. Not only for themselves, but for the eventual good of the entire school and for the whole town of Dixboro. I am confident that if the Board approves this plan, Dixboro will gain in three ways.

We'll have a new elementary school gym in a very few years. We'll have teams that win more consistently. And we'll have a more prosperous community."

Mr. Slade stopped and consulted his watch. "Now, I hope we can move along to a favorable decision." He looked around as if daring anyone to speak up.

"One question, Mr. Slade." The speaker rose from his seat near the front of the hall. It was Tom Joyce.

Mr. Slade nodded curtly.

"I find myself in complete agreement with most of the things you've said. But there's one point I can't quite shake off."

"What's that?"

"It has to do with means. I don't quarrel with your ends. I think everyone here wants the same things for Dixboro as you do. But I think in this case, the ends don't justify such drastic means."

"I'm not quite sure I understand you," Mr. Slade said uncertainly.

"I'll see if I can't make it clearer," Tom said. "You propose to turn the elementary school gym over to the Midgets for their exclusive use. Is that correct?"

"Only for a season and only as an experiment," Mr. Slade explained.

"If the experiment is successful, you'll continue it?"

"Yes," Mr. Slade admitted. "But only for a few years. By that time we hope to have raised enough money for a new gym that's large enough to accommodate everybody."

"But during those years, your plan shuts everybody out of the gym except one group of boys."

"If we keep it open to everybody, nobody will be able to use it properly."

"I might go along with that, Mr. Slade, except for one thing. The group has already been chosen. Nobody else can get in."

"Oh, come now, Mr. Joyce," Dan's father said impatiently. "You know enough about basketball to realize that when a team has been playing together they shouldn't be broken up. These boys organized themselves. I think we ought to give them a chance."

"I think we ought to give everybody a chance," Tom said firmly.

"How?" Mr. Slade flared. "Where? There's no more available space in Dixboro."

"Yes, there is," Tom said quietly.

This stopped Mr. Slade cold. He looked around at his fellow Board members in confusion and then turned back to Tom. "Could you tell us where it is?"

"I'd be happy to. Before the new Alumni Gym was built in Dixboro we used what is now the second cafeteria. But it's still a gym."

Mr. Slade laughed. "What about the tables and chairs?"

"They're movable."

"Who'd move them?"

"The boys. If they want to play badly enough, they'll fold away the tables and chairs and set them up again after practice."

"And if they don't?" Mr. Slade challenged.

"If they don't, they don't deserve the chance and I'll go along with you. But the important thing is to give them that chance."

Win looked around at his neighbors. They were all listening intently and several of them were agreeing with what Tom said.

"I have a question, Mr. Joyce." This came from Superintendent Chalmers. "Who is going to supervise their play? Who is going to take responsibility for their presence in the building? All of your afternoons are completely filled with Varsity and Junior Varsity practice. I'm afraid we can't hire another coach especially for one group of boys."

Mr. Slade broke into a triumphant smile. "Yes, Mr. Joyce. How do you plan to meet that objection?"

"This person we need would have to be responsible and know something about basketball. Is that right?"

Both Slade and Chalmers nodded.

"Would you consider a member of my Varsity basketball squad? A boy with a keen knowledge of the sport and a strong sense of responsibility?"

The two men on the platform looked at each other uncertainly. "Well . . ." Chalmers began.

"I think that might be acceptable," Mr. Slade interrupted coldly. "Provided you can find such a volunteer."

"If I can, will you agree to turn over the high school cafeteria for the use I've described?"

"You mean to turn it over to a gang of young boys so they can play basketball?" Mr. Slade's manner was clearly hostile.

Tom bridled at the implied insult. "I don't understand," he said sharply, "the difference between the gang of boys you're promoting and another gang. They're all students at the elementary school, aren't they?"

"Yes," Mr. Slade admitted.

"And they're all sons of the people of Dixboro." Tom's voice rang out in a strong indictment. "I'm not trying to destroy your plan, but you seem to be determined to destroy mine. I do not happen to believe in favoritism—especially in sports. If you create an opportunity, it should be available to everyone. Even if it means extra work and extra planning. I'm firmly convinced that I can find at least one boy on the Varsity basketball squad who thinks it is as important as I do."

There was scattered applause throughout the auditorium as Tom finished, and its meaning was not lost on Mr. Slade.

"All right," he said stonily. "Your proposal will be put before the Board. Who's your candidate for coach?"

"Win Hadley," Tom said clearly.

There was a hushed gasp of surprise.

"Is he present tonight?"

"I believe so." Tom turned and scanned the auditorium. "Win?" he called.

Win felt himself flush nervously as he stood up to meet the curious stares of several hundred people. But his voice was firm when he spoke. "Here I am," he said.

Mr. Slade fixed him with an icy stare. "You understand, young man, what you are letting yourself in for?"

"I think so, sir," Win answered.

"You will be responsible for every boy in your charge. I might as well warn you that you'll be held accountable for the slightest irregularity and that, if any occurs, all privileges will be immediately canceled."

"I understand, sir," Win replied.

"Very well, then. We'll take a vote on the two proposals."

He turned his back abruptly and stalked over to his place at the end of the table opposite Dr. Chalmers.

CHAPTER ELEVEN

Plain Talk

NEWS OF WHAT HAD HAPPENED at the School Board meeting traveled fast. By nine o'clock the next morning Win had already answered three calls from friends who wanted to know if it was true about his coaching a second elementary school team. The fourth call was from Matt.

"Hi, Coach!" Matt boomed out. "I thought you were going to get in touch with me yesterday."

"I'm sorry about that," Win answered, "but I got tied up."

"You sure did! Is all this something you and Tom Joyce dreamed up together?"

"Well, sort of," Win admitted. "He asked me if I wanted to do it and I said yes. I don't know why everybody's so excited. It's not even a team. Just a bunch of kids working out."

Matt chuckled softly and Win could almost see him shaking his head. "That may be your story, but it's not the way I heard it. People are saying it's a direct slap at Mr. Slade and just another round in the running fight between Tom Joyce and Joe Harsh."

"It's got nothing to do with that, Matt!" Win declared hotly. "I don't see why . . ."

"Hey, take it easy," Matt interrupted in an injured tone. "I'm on your side. Remember?"

"Sorry."

"Well, okay. I just wanted to let you know the score and get you braced for a blast from our old buddy."

"Who do you mean?"

"Neal Travers, natch. I'll bet a couple of doughnuts he's got a blistering column all lined up for tomorrow."

It turned out that Matt was right. The events at the meeting had made a big enough splash for the story to appear on the front page of Monday's paper. Win saw that it was written by Neal Travers.

DIXBORO BOARD TAKES FIRST STEP TOWARD
NEW ELEMENTARY SCHOOL GYM
Meeting, First Marred by
Objections, Ends with Compromise

It was Tom Joyce, coach of the Dixboro Cougars, vs. Owen Slade and the almost unanimous sentiment of the town last Saturday night in the latest development of a running dogfight between Dixboro's athletic mentor and Joe Harsh, head man of the newly formed Midgets.

At a regularly scheduled meeting of the School Board, which, incidentally, usually attracts nothing more controversial than a couple of polite yawns from Dixboro's citizens but which, Saturday night, played to standing-room-only crowds, Owen Slade and Tom Joyce engaged in a debate over the merits of letting the Midgets use the facilities of the present, hopelessly crowded elementary school gym. Both sides won.

The Midgets got the gym and Dixboro got a second elementary school team that is yet unnamed but will work out in the old cafeteria of the high school which, you may remember, used to be the gym.

This second team is the brain wave of Tom Joyce, who promptly dumped all coaching duties into the inexperienced lap of Win Hadley, potential star member of this year's Cougar Quintet.

One of Joyce's objections to Joe Harsh was that he taught the wrong kind of ball. So then what does the old master do? He hands a bunch of youngsters over to a lad who has never taught any kind of ball—right or wrong.

The logic of this escapes your observer, even

though the purpose is clear—another attempt to discredit Harsh by forming a second team which will use the Joyce method of teaching basketball by proxy.

A game between these two teams is inevitable and should be scheduled as soon as possible. For one thing, it will let Dixboro's basketball fans see both men in action and give them a fair basis on which to make their decision—for Joyce or for Harsh.

For another, it may help clear the air and give the Cougars a chance to get back to the main business at hand, which is playing and trying to win basketball games. Win Hadley, please note. Do you really think you're helping the team by pretending to be a coach?

All this is by way of underscoring a little-noticed fact. Dixboro's first game of the season will get under way at 7:30 Wednesday night. If anybody cares, see you there.

There were further details of what happened at the meeting on the inside pages of the paper, but Win didn't bother to read them. He was out of the house before eight o'clock on his way to an early appointment with Tom Joyce and the school caretaker to discuss the most efficient way of removing tables and chairs from the cafeteria floor.

Classes kept him occupied until lunch and then came a meeting with Tommy Burton who prom-

ised to show up for the first practice on Thursday
—the day after the season opener with Framton.

Varsity practice later that afternoon was quiet
and tense. Tom Joyce had prepared elaborate
scouting notes on Framton and dragged out the
board to diagram them. After the chalk talk, the
Junior Varsity walked through several of Framton's key plays while the Varsity went through the
motions of setting up the most effective defense
to stop them.

"Framton," Tom told his players, "has got the
big advantage of height. Their center, Jud Scott,
is six foot seven if he's an inch. He'll be your baby,
Boots. I think you can stop him because Scott can't
jump. As a matter of fact, the team as a whole is
a little clumsy. Because of that, a lot of writers have
dismissed Framton as a second-rate ball club. I
think they've made a mistake. These boys play
with desire and they're always in there trying.
I've seen a lot of basketball in my day and there's
one thing I've noticed. The team that wants to
win usually does." Tom paused, stared at his
players thoughtfully and put aside his piece of
chalk.

"That leads me to something I've been wanting
to talk about for a few days now." He plunged his
hands into his pockets and slowly walked up and
down before the stands. "I've known most of you

fellows for years. I've watched you play and I've watched you fight for a spot on this squad. But now, in the last week or so, I've watched you lose your drive and—much as I hate to say it—your will to win." He took a deep breath and ran his eye over the squad. There was nothing unfriendly in the look he gave them, but it was the expression of a troubled man.

"We might as well come right out and talk about it," Tom said finally. "Everyone else in town does it, and I've never thought much of pretending things are all right when they're not. Neal Travers and some of the people in Dixboro seem to think that I'm obsessed with this fellow Joe Harsh. They claim that everything I do is directed against him —that I've forgotten about the team and neglected my job as coach."

Tom resumed his thoughtful pacing. "I can't help what they think and, of course, they're entitled to their own opinions. But here, for whatever it's worth, is exactly the way I really feel. I don't like Joe Harsh because I don't like the kind of basketball he's teaching. That's true. But I've never opposed the idea of a Midget team. My only concern was that every boy in the elementary school should have a chance to play. When I found the squad was closed, I felt it was my duty to give other boys a similar chance. I won't be coaching that team. As a matter of fact, I won't have a thing to do with it. I'm not interested in showing up Joe Harsh and I don't care if the two teams never meet. Now that a second playing area has been found, my only interest is in coaching you fellows the best way I know and seeing you in there trying all the time. That's why your attitude worries me. I've been frank with you and I'd like your side of it. Anybody care to speak up?"

Tom's eyes roamed hopefully over the silent group of basketball players, but there was no response to his invitation. Dan Slade, Red McGinley, Larry Jensen and three or four others sat staring stonily down at the court, refusing to meet Tom's glance.

After an uncomfortable pause of a few seconds, Tom turned and pushed the blackboard beyond the side lines. "All right," he said in a brisk and businesslike voice, "form three lanes and let's have some passing with some snap to it. I want to hear lots of holler. Let's go!"

The squad sorted itself out and began the drill Tom had ordered. Despite attempts by Win, Matt, Boots and a half dozen others, the passing was listless and uninspired. A sullen air of resentment seemed to hang over the court and this acted like a stifling blanket over the spirits of the players. After about ten minutes, Tom blew his whistle.

"Excused," he said curtly. "Light workout to-morrow at three-thirty. Then I'll want you all to eat an early supper and lie down afterward. I don't care if you can't sleep, just so long as you're on your back and trying to relax. Game time is seven-thirty, and you're to report no later than six-thirty and be ready to come out on the court at seven-fifteen. I'll have the starting line-up posted on the bulletin board tomorrow. That's all for now."

Tom turned on his heel without a smile and strode off the court through a door that led to his office.

The players silently trooped off in the other direction, talking in low murmurs. They looked, Win thought to himself, like a bunch of boys headed for a funeral and certainly not like a team headed for a championship.

CHAPTER TWELVE

Season's Start

"BETTER HAVE WHITEY tape it first." The advice came from Tom Joyce who was watching Win tie a guard around his left knee. The big clock over the door read twenty minutes to seven, but already the locker room was crowded with players, hurriedly suiting up.

"It hasn't been bothering me recently," Win replied.

"That pad won't give you much support and we can't afford to take chances."

Win nodded, slipped off the guard and walked over to the rubbing table where Whitey Comstock was carefully taping a pair of ankles that belonged to Boots Lohman.

Boots was protesting mildly. "Take it easy, Whitey," he said. "I'd like a little blood to circulate down there."

"I know what I'm doing," Whitey grunted as he gave the tape another expert twist. "You athletes are all alike. You think you know my job better than I do." He snapped the hook into place and gave Boots a friendly slap on the backside. "On your feet, big boy, and see how it feels."

Boots rolled off the table and took a few experimental hops. "Great!" he said. "Just right."

"See what I mean!" Whitey said. "If I'd made it any looser, you'd have hollered that it wasn't any good. Now go out there and play the game of your life." He turned to Win. "You next?"

"Yep."

"Well, climb on up then." He peered down at Win's left knee. "You want a tape job fitted for that pad, eh?"

When Win nodded, Whitey went to work skillfully and quickly, grumbling bitterly at the delicate condition of modern athletes. "In my day," he said, "we never even heard of a pulled tendon. We'd have been ashamed to go out there with all these bandages you young fellows wear. I expect in a couple o' years they'll be using colored bandages and you'll all look like gift wrapping under a Christmas tree."

Win smiled at Whitey's muttered blast. It was all part of a routine that he had come to know and appreciate as Whitey's way of relaxing the boys before game time. He felt a light punch on his leg.

"You're all set, boy." Whitey gripped his shoulder and gave it an encouraging shake. "You're going to play a whale of a game tonight," he said. "I can tell."

"I hope so," Win replied as he moved back to his locker. This was the tough part. The waiting. He lowered himself down on the hardwood bench that ran in front of the lockers and tried to ease the mounting tension in his body. But it didn't work.

Above him he could hear the echoing rumble of the crowds as they slowly filled the stands. It was a sellout house that night with better than three thousand fans expected. Win had never played in front of so many people before except in football. But that was different. The stands seemed miles away and the teams weren't enclosed under the same roof with the fans. He tried to imagine what Alumni Gym looked like with three thousand people packed along its sides. After a while he gave it up and just listened.

There was an abrupt roar from the crowd and Win could hear the band salute Framton with their marching song. He opened one eye and took a look at the clock. Right on schedule. Framton was taking the floor at seven o'clock for preliminary warm-up. Fifteen more minutes. From up above came the noise of hundreds of stamping feet and an occasional burst of applause. Win closed his eyes and concentrated on the Framton team.

Aside from Jud Scott, their six-foot-seven-inch center, Framton boasted a superb set-shot artist in Harry Evers, their left guard. Pete Andrucci, their other guard, was a pretty fair playmaker and the only man with speed to spare. Budd Arnold, the left forward, had a neat jump shot and Charlie Halverson, a blond boy of Swedish extraction, possessed a deadly hook shot.

Charlie was Win's responsibility, and Tom Joyce had given him detailed instructions on how to play him. "Keep away from him," Tom had said. "Give yourself some air. He'll try to make actual contact with you so he can feel which way you're going. Then he'll feint, reverse, and pop in that hook of his. But if he doesn't know how you're going to move, he'll be tied up in knots." It made sense to Win and he planned his strategy accordingly.

As he was reviewing the Framton squad in his mind's eye, a hand reached down and gave his head a friendly tousle. "Hi, Sleeping Beauty. How're you feeling?" It was Matt, grinning happily from ear to ear.

Win swung around to a sitting position and looked at Matt enviously. The big guard seemed completely unaffected by the usual pre-game attack of nerves. "How do you do it, Matt?" he sighed. "You look as if you didn't have a care in the world."

"Well, I don't," Matt observed philosophically, sitting down beside Win. "The worries are all up there." He pointed overhead in the direction of the gym. "And they won't be starting for another half hour yet."

Win grinned and started to answer, but just then the door to Tom Joyce's office opened and the coach entered. The talk in the locker room quieted down immediately.

"We have five minutes, fellows. Just long enough for me to wish you luck and read off the starting five in case any of you didn't look at the bulletin board." There was a low chuckle around the room at that. "We'll start with Hadley, Slade, Lohman, Parsons and Walsh. Boots, you're captain, so you'll be directing strategy out there. I want you to call a time-out right after Framton's first basket, then huddle around the bench. I may want to call some fresh signals. But for now, we'll start the ball rolling with our old style. When we switch to a more open game, Hadley will move up to play left forward and Walsh will drop back to guard. Okay?"

"Time," Whitey warned, glancing at the clock.

Tom shoved some papers in his pocket and grinned at his squad. "All right, fellows. Let's take them. I think you know every one of their tricks. Up we go!"

Win climbed the steps leading to the gym on rubbery legs. None of the players were talking much, and all around, Win could hear the short intake of dry, nervous breathing. Someone shoved a basketball in his hand, and the next instant Tom Joyce threw open the door. "Let's go, boys!" he shouted. "Let's show them we mean business!"

With a ragged yell, the team surged out into the blinding light of the huge gym. The crowd thundered its appreciation as the band struck up the "Dixboro Fight Song." Flashbulbs popped from the stands and everywhere there was a blur of color and a confusion of noise.

The Dixboro team formed passing and shooting lines under several baskets and worked for several minutes to get the stiffness out of their joints. A blast from the whistle brought them over to their bench, and as the crowd stilled respectfully and everyone stood at attention, the band broke into the national anthem.

A second blast and the starting players peeled off their jackets, handed them to the manager who came bustling up to receive them, then formed a quick huddle for the pre-game grip.

"Here we go, fellows," Boots Lohman growled. "Number one for us. I think I can get the tap. I'll try to feed it to you, Win."

Win nodded and ran lightly out to take his place on the court. Charlie Halverson, the Framton right forward, joined him, and the two boys shook hands.

"How have you been, Win?" the blond youngster asked with a smile. "Knee all better?"

"One hundred per cent, Charlie," Win assured him. "I'm going to try to run rings around you."

"And I'll try to stop you," Charlie grinned back. "Here's luck to us both."

"Right."

The referee's whistle blew sharply, and Alumni Gym quieted for the first play of the Dixboro basketball season.

Boots timed his jump perfectly and Win was able to get a half step on Charlie Halverson. The next instant he had the ball and was dribbling past the center court toward Dan Slade. Dan neatly feinted his man out of position and Win rifled him a quick pass.

The Framton defense saw the play coming and closed in on the tall forward. Win put on the brakes, watched Charlie Halverson fly past him, and waited confidently for Dan to return the pass for an easy set shot.

But Dan elected to drive in for the score. With

three Framton players on his back, he dribbled to the basket and went up for the shot.

He was never even able to get the ball out of his hands. Harry Evers went right up with him and twisted the ball cleanly away. Evers landed lightly and drifted off to find a receiver, but before he could move three steps, Dan Slade lunged out in a desperate attempt to regain possession of the ball. As Dan's groping hands closed over Harry's arm, the ball squirted out into the middle of the court where it was stopped by the referee. A single whistle blast called the foul and halted the action. Harry took his shot and sank it without trouble.

Tony Parsons grabbed the ball, shoved it into the referee's hand and moved beyond the out-of-play line. He passed off to Win who moved it on up to Boots Lohman. Boots took it into the slot and lobbed a high one to Dan Slade just as Tony Parsons broke into the clear.

Again Dan tried for the shot. This time it was a hook that didn't come off properly because Budd Arnold had moved in from behind to put on the squeeze. The ball bounced crazily against the backboard and was snared by Jud Scott who was standing alone waiting for it.

Jud wheeled and rifled a long pass to Pete Andrucci who was sprinting for the Dixboro basket at top speed. Win saw the pass coming and took off after him, but the sturdy Framton guard was able to put it through the cords with an east bank shot.

"Time!" Boots Lohman bellowed, leading the way over to the bench in front of Tom Joyce. As the players knelt in a loose semicircle around him, Tom spoke quickly, spitting the words out like bullets. "They're using a collapsing defense," he said. "Every time you get the ball into their court, the guards fall all over you like a blanket. That means no inside shooting. When you forwards get the ball," he said, nodding toward Dan and Ed Walsh, "wait until the defense closes in on you and fire it right back out to the center for a set shot."

Dan looked at him with a frown. "You mean you don't want us to shoot at all?" he asked.

Tom nodded. "That's right. What good does it do? You can't even get the ball away."

Further instructions were cut short by the warning horn and the game was resumed. Win put the ball into play this time with a high, hard pass to Tony Parsons. Tony handed off to Boots and then moved in front of him to act as a screen. Boots feinted once, broke for the basket and shot a bounce pass to Ed Walsh.

Immediately three players converged on Ed. He avoided them neatly, saw Win standing in the clear and gave him a perfect pass. Win dropped it through for Dixboro's first score.

"That's the stuff!" Boots hollered as he back-pedaled into defense. Win grinned over to him and got set to cover Charlie Halverson.

The Framton five came up the court with surprising speed, moving the ball back and forth in a well-practiced figure-eight pattern. Win remembered Tom Joyce once saying that the main trouble with a set-pass pattern was that the opposition could always predict the next receiver. After the maneuver had been completed twice, Win saw what the pattern was. Charlie Halverson was the fourth player to get the ball. It went from Andrucci to Jud Scott, over to Budd Arnold who handed off to Charlie. Charlie then had the option of trying his hook, giving to Harry Evers for a set shot, or returning to Andrucci to start the cycle all over again.

Poising himself, Win saw the ball whip to Jud. The bounce pass went to Budd Arnold who faked a shot. If he was right, the next pass would go to Halverson.

Win took a chance and made his move. He heard Halverson's shout of warning, but it was too late. The ball floated into Win's hand and he was off. He felt pursuers pounding up the court behind him and hooked a one-hander over to Dan Slade on his left. Everyone on the court fully expected Dan to follow through with his drive toward the basket, but Dan drew up and fired a long set shot from center court. There was a gasp of astonishment from the crowd. The ball hung in the air, fell to the rim and bounced away.

From where he was standing, Win saw Dan shake himself angrily before he tore down the court toward Jud Scott who had retrieved the ball. As Jud reared back for a pass, Dan vaulted forward and slammed his shoulder against the big center's arm. An angry blast of the whistle called down Dan's second personal foul.

After Jud eased the ball through the rim for Framton's fourth point, Boots said something to Dan under his breath. Dan took a step toward the big center and muttered angrily. Win barely caught the words, "He told me not to shoot from the inside, didn't he?" The next instant he was gone.

Boots shook his head and shuffled over to receive Tony Parsons' pass. This time, Dixboro's offense ignored Dan Slade and kept the ball on Ed Walsh's side of the court. The strategy netted them a second two-pointer, sunk by Win a few steps back of the free-throw line.

By this time, however, Framton was aware of the dissension in the Dixboro ranks and switched over to a rattling game. They pressed both Ed Walsh and Dan Slade mercilessly, forcing them to make errors that cost Dixboro at least half a dozen points. By the time the quarter ended, Dan Slade had been charged with three personal fouls and Ed Walsh, two. The score read Framton 12, Dixboro 6.

In the time-out huddle between quarters, Boots tried to rally the team. "Let's take it easy, fellows," he soothed. "Don't be so anxious, Dan. All you have to do is throw it back out to us."

"Sure," Dan snarled. "So the coach's pet here—" he jerked a thumb in Win's direction—"can dump it in for a score. Why don't we all quit and let him play the game alone!"

Boots scowled, but before he had a chance to reply, Matt Hughes dropped down beside them. "Nice game, Ed," he grinned, patting Ed Walsh on the arm. "Take a breather for a couple of minutes."

Ed looked up in surprise, a flush of resentment coloring his face. He started to say something, changed his mind and stalked stiff-legged over to the bench.

"New line-up," Matt informed them, resting easily on one knee. "Win and Dan switch. I'll be in Ed's spot. Same strategy. Feed it to us and when they collapse in, we'll hand it back to you. Okay?"

The referee's whistle cut off further talk and Win moved over to play his new position. He reflected that Dan had nothing to complain about.

Now he was in the spot to do the scoring—and that was the way he liked it. Well, that was okay with Win, too, if it helped the team.

At the whistle, Tony fed to Boots who dribbled over to form a screen for Dan. The rangy blond cut sharply for the basket and loosed a perfect one-handed to Matt in the corner. As expected, the Framton defense fell back and Matt was surrounded by three guards. But Matt wasn't trying for the shot. He managed a surprise bounce pass to Win who saw the two remaining Framton players close in on him. That left three Dixboro players in the clear. Dan was closest, so Win rifled him a pass and watched with satisfaction as Dan sank an easy set shot.

There was a murmur of approval from the crowd at this neatly executed play that quickly swelled into a prolonged roar as Dixboro followed through with four more two-pointers—three of them by Dan and the fourth by Boots Lohman.

Both Matt and Win were performing masterfully under the basket with their fancy playmaking and ball juggling that kept the Framton five off balance long enough to let one of the Dixboro sharpshooters pour it in from the outside. On defense they covered their men effectively and managed to snare two deceptions.

After Boots sank the fourth goal, Framton called

for time and the Dixboro quintet threw themselves down on the court beside Tom Joyce.

"Nice going," Tom told them approvingly. "We've got them on the run. Only five minutes to the half. But now, watch out for a switch. Their collapsing defense isn't working so they may try a two-one-two zone. If they do, that's easy. You can run them off the floor. Instead of feeding to the outside, try the fast break and hand-off. The inside men'll do most of the shooting." He glanced up at the sound of the horn. "Good luck."

Tom had called the turn perfectly. Framton changed over to the more cautious zone defense with most of the pressure up front. Boots took off from Tony, reversed his field and passed to Dan. When he saw Dan with the ball, Win broke for the basket, hoping for a pass. Instead, Dan tried to dribble through a scissor play and lost the ball. The referee's whistle stopped the scramble that followed and called Dan's fourth personal foul. One more and he would be out of the game.

Before the line-up for the free throw, there was a second horn. Win glanced over at the scorer's table and saw Teddy Scholari report. Teddy checked with the referee who nodded. "Scholari for Slade," he announced. "Framton has one free throw."

Dan stiffened with surprise and walked over to

the bench. Win could see the muscles in his neck tighten and bunch in anger.

The Dixboro rooters groaned slightly as Jud Scott whistled his toss through the cords, then set up an encouraging cheer for Dixboro. But the Cougar attack had lost its punch. Time and again the offense fizzled under the Framton basket with missed chances or poorly set up shots. At the half-time buzzer, Framton was out in front 32–19. The Dixboro team looked at the numbers in amazement. Framton was supposed to be a pushover—a warm-up game for the season. Silently they followed Tom Joyce down into the locker room.

Despite a vigorous pep talk and a clear blueprint of attack provided by Tom Joyce, the second half was no improvement over the first. Once or twice the Cougars caught fire, but they were unable to sustain their drive. Framton's steady play pushed them further out in front until, in the last quarter, with less than four minutes remaining, the numbers on the big board read: Framton 49, Dixboro 35.

At that point, Win suddenly exploded with three quick tallies. After a hurried time out, Framton double-teamed Win in an attempt to hold him down. But Win refused to be stopped. He was all over the court, dragging two and sometimes three Framton players with him, finding loopholes in a smothering defense. Whenever he couldn't make the shot himself, he passed off to Boots or Tony or Matt.

Win's sparkling play touched off pandemonium in the stands. Framton called two time-outs in a row, hoping to map an effective defense strategy. Win promptly sank a long set shot to bring the score to 51-47.

His shot brought the fans to their feet, cheering wildly. In the confusion that followed, the referee's whistle was heard and two figures made their way to the scoring table. Win glanced at the clock. With forty seconds to play, Tom Joyce was gambling on Ed Walsh and Dan Slade.

The two boys took their positions as Boots fired a quick one over to Tony Parsons. The old reliables of last year's team drove up the middle, broke cross court, then cut down the sides. As Boots charged by, Win picked him up, hoping to screen him from Framton's defenders. The screen was only partially effective and Win saw that Boots wouldn't be able to make the shot. He slipped out of the pack around Boots and flashed toward the basket. The pass from Boots was high and perfectly timed. Win's fingers held the ball for a second, then pushed it up against the backboard for the score that made it 51-49.

Two more points and twenty seconds to go.

The Framton rooters in the stands were yelling for the team to freeze the ball.

"Get it! Get the ball!" came the cry from the Dixboro side. Both benches had empties as the players lined up along the court, shouting encouragement to their teammates.

Jud Scott brought the ball slowly upcourt, keeping one eye on the clock. Fifteen seconds. Win knew an interception was the only chance and he watched the pass pattern like a hawk.

In the end it was Boots Lohman who got the ball. His long arm snaked out and deflected a pass intended for Pete Andrucci. Win saw the ball bounce unsteadily toward the side lines and lunged out to snare it before it rolled out of play. Leaning down, he scooped it up at full gallop and was immediately hemmed in by two Framton guards.

Out of the corner of his eye, Win saw a flash of black and gold in the clear and let fly with a desperation heave that struck squarely on target. The player with the ball now was Dan Slade and a frantic Framton defense converged on him.

Win's guards deserted him to race to the new point of danger. That left the entire Dixboro team in the clear. Gleefully, they pounded up the court, waiting for the pass.

Dan dribbled, faked to his left and eluded one defender. Win looked at the clock. Ten seconds.

"Pass!" he breathed to himself. "Pass!"

Dan shook off another Framton player and advanced several more steps.

"Pass!" Someone yelled from the stands. The crowd took up the urgent chant: "Pass! Pass! Pass!" they pleaded.

But Dan was determined to thread his way through the entire Framton team. He slipped through another hole and shot a quick look at the clock. Five seconds.

Now only Jud Scott stood between Dan and the basket. Three seconds. Dan tried to break and reverse, but Jud hung on grimly. Dan saw he didn't have time for another maneuver and stopped his forward motion. As the crowd held its breath, he gathered himself for a shot. It was an impossibly long chance, but for a moment Win thought it would succeed.

The ball described a graceful arc, high above Jud Scott's waving hands, flew straight for the backboard, bounced once, settled on the rim and fell harmlessly away. Boots leaped for the rebound, but before he could get the ball off, the horn sounded.

Framton had won by a score of 51-49.

CHAPTER THIRTEEN

Bad News

COUGAR STRATEGY BACKFIRES AS
FRAMTON DUMPS DIXBORO, 51-49

Well, it happened. Framton won. Take a closer look at the score. Those figures tell a significant story. Framton managed to squeak out a victory by the bare margin of two points, and the club was trying its best. Dixboro, playing confused and rattled ball, almost won. There's no question about it, Dixboro has the better team. Then why didn't they win?

Here are some more questions to ponder. Why did Coach Tom Joyce yank Dan Slade early in the second quarter? The flashy hoop star had just tallied with eight points in three short minutes of play. You don't usually bench a hot performer. But Coach Joyce did. Why?

This reporter interviewed Dan Slade after the game

and this is what he told me. "I don't know," the tall, blond youngster said slowly. He was obviously troubled by what had happened. "I can't seem to do anything right. The whole squad seems to be mixed up."

Right you are, Dan. It is mixed up. Here's another question. Win Hadley hit the target last night for 24 points. That's just one short of half the team total. Tom Joyce says that basketball is a team game. If so, how come one man does so much scoring?

Here's what Joe Harsh, an interested observer in the stands, had to say about it: "That's easy. The team had orders to feed the ball to Hadley. He was the only one allowed to take a shot." Why?

Harsh had an opinion on that, too: "It's Hadley's reward for being a good boy . . . for going along with Tom Joyce on this second elementary team."

And there you have it. The story behind the story of Dixboro's defeat. But will Tom Joyce do anything about it? Well, that's a question that will soon be answered. The Cougars have two more home games scheduled before a three-game road tour. Friday night they meet Butler Academy at Alumni Gym and on Monday night they face Wharton Tech for their first Conference tilt. The Cougars can afford to lose to Butler, but Wharton Tech is a must.

We'll see what happens. Meanwhile, tennis, anyone?

Tom Joyce called a surprise meeting of the Varsity basketball squad in his office during the lunch period. The announcement came over the school's public address system at ten-thirty.

Apprehensively, the players gathered to hear what Tom had to say. It was short and to the point. He strode into the room, nodded in greeting and placed a copy of the *Crawford Record* on his desk.

"I assume you've read the account of last night's game?" There was a general bobbing of heads and Tom continued. "As members of the Varsity basketball squad you are—or should be—familiar with the rules governing the relation between Dixboro athletes and the press. All requests for personal interviews are to be referred to me or to the principal for clearance. We've explained the reason many times. It's because we don't like the idea of reporters making a star out of any individual player. In special cases, we'll allow an interview, but we always insist on knowing about it in advance."

Tom leaned against the desk and looked at Dan Slade. "Did Neal Travers ask you for your views on last night's game?"

Dan flushed and tried to return Tom's questioning stare. "Yes, sir," he said finally.

"Did you grant him the interview?"

Dan squared his shoulders and looked Tom straight in the eye. "Yes, I did."

"And what he printed in the paper here—" Tom pointed to Neal Travers' column—"is that what you said?"

"Pretty much. I don't remember—"

Tom picked up the paper. "Do you remember telling him that the whole squad seems 'mixed up'?"

"I don't think I used exactly those words."

"But that's what you meant?" Tom fired the question sharply.

"I—I guess so," Dan faltered, dropping his glance to the floor.

There was a long pause in the room. Tom fingered the paper absent-mindedly and sighed. "The best I was hoping for," he said softly, "was a mistake. I hoped that somehow Travers had twisted your words to make you say something you hadn't intended." He straightened up and spoke out in a firm voice. "In that case, Dan, I have no alternative left me but to suspend you from the squad for five days."

There was a muted gasp of astonishment at this news. Tom continued evenly. "That means you'll miss the next two games. I'm sorry about that. We could have used you." He turned and spoke to the rest of the players. "I called you in here just now because I wanted it clearly understood why Dan is being suspended. This will probably cause some comment in the newspaper and so I've put together a statement for Neal Travers. I plan to send it to him and that should be the end of it. But," he added wryly, "I'm sure it won't be. If Travers or anyone else even remotely connected with the *Record* approaches you for a comment, refer them to me. Is that clear?"

The boys nodded and Tom dismissed them. "Report to practice next Tuesday afternoon," he told Dan Slade as he left. "Until then, don't bother to show up."

As the silent boys trooped out of Tom Joyce's office, they almost instinctively broke into two separate groups. Ed Walsh went over to Dan Slade and began talking in a low voice. Dan, frowning darkly, nodded, and together the two boys drifted away. Before long, several of the other players followed them.

"What do you think?" Matt muttered out of the side of his mouth.

Win shook his head. "I don't know. I wish I knew what was behind all this."

"Me too," Matt replied. "I can't figure what Travers thinks he's doing."

"Maybe he'll give us a hint in his next column."

Matt gave a short laugh. "I doubt it. He'll be too

busy tearing into Tom Joyce for suspending Dan Slade."

"And as usual twisting the facts to suit his own purpose," Win added bitterly.

"I wonder how many people in this town believe Neal Travers," Matt mused. "Can't they see that Tom had to suspend him? He couldn't allow him to break the rules like that."

"I know," Win said. "But think of the howl if we drop the next two games. As Tom said, we sure could use Dan against Wharton Tech."

"And Butler's no snap either," Matt pointed out.

Win nodded glumly. "No use crying over it. It's done. We'll have to get along without him."

"Think we can do it?"

Win shrugged. "Ask me next week. We'll know then. Meanwhile, I've got a job to do."

"What's that?" Matt asked in surprise.

Win looked at him with a smile. "Tommy Burton and the boys," he said. "Don't tell me you'd forgotten!"

Matt grinned. "Say, that's right! You start your first practice today! Mind if I come along?"

"Glad to have you. Maybe you can help."

"Sure thing. Let's go."

When they arrived at the cafeteria that afternoon, they found Tommy Burton and about a dozen other boys busily stacking chairs and tables. It was a scene of noisy but organized confusion, with Tommy directing traffic and bellowing out orders. At last a playing area was cleared. Tommy consulted the clock on the wall and nodded approvingly. "Ten minutes and thirty seconds," he announced. "It'll go a lot faster next time." He turned to Win and said expectantly, "All set, Coach. Want me to call the fellows?"

Win nodded and Tommy let loose with a shrill whistle. "Gather 'round, everybody," he ordered. "Listen," he said as the boys jostled around him. "We've been talking it over and we thought up a name for our team."

"Great," Win said. "What's it going to be?"

"Well, it's this way," Tommy explained. "If Freddie Slade is going to call his bunch the Midgets, we've gotta have something to top that. Right?"

"Check."

"Okay then. We're gonna be the Giants."

Win caught Matt's eye and winked. "That sounds wonderful, Tommy," he said seriously. "You going to get uniforms?"

"You bet!" Tommy cried. "Everybody's gotta pay a quarter a week if they want to play."

"Let's see now," Matt said. "At that rate you'll have your uniforms by—er—" He glanced up at

the ceiling for a hurried bout of mental arith-
metic.

"Two years from February," Tommy answered
promptly.

Win fought to suppress a smile. "But, Tommy,
he said gently, "by that time you'll be playing in
high school. You won't need them."

Tommy's face fell. "Gee," he said. "I never
thought of that."

"Well, who needs uniforms anyway!" Win cried.
"Let's worry about that later."

"Okay," Tommy replied happily. "What do we
do first?"

"First of all," Win told them, "sit down. We're
going to start from the ground up. I'm going to
pretend you don't even know what a basketball
looks like."

The boys settled obediently on the floor and
Win launched into his lecture on the fundamentals
of basketball play. Time and again he caught himself echoing phrases that Tom Joyce had used. At
first he thought he should try to be original, but
later on he realized that Tom had said it just
about the best possible way.

The Giants responded eagerly to everything,
their young faces absorbed by Win's words. After
a skull session and a demonstration, Win put them
through some basic drills. At the end of that, he

excused them, helped them put back the cafeteria tables and chairs, and rushed off to get ready for Varsity practice.

"I think they're going to be great," Matt said enthusiastically as the two boys suited up in the locker room.

Win agreed. "They learn fast," he said.

"You sure got yourself a team," Matt told him as they made their way up the stairs to the gym. "I wish we had one with half as much spirit."

There was no comment made about Dan's absence from practice that afternoon. But it was clear that the suspension had made a deep impression. The team played shakily, with little assurance and none of the pep and vigor that go along with winning teams. Tom Joyce excused them finally and retired to the privacy of his office where he experimented with juggling line-ups, hoping to salvage at least some of the pieces. Neal Travers' column in the *Crawford Record* the next morning was the most vitriolic to date. He protested Dan's suspension and raged at Tom Joyce for decreeing it. He even demanded Tom's resignation as athletic director of the school, charging that Tom was destroying the Cougars as a basketball force.

Win had prepared himself for the usual Travers treatment and refused to let himself get upset by it. But some of the boys on the squad, notably

Boots Lohman and Tony Parsons, were bitter at the kind of stuff Travers was dishing out. The light workout before the Butler game that afternoon was charged with an atmosphere of resentment and anger. The players acted like strangers with none of the usual lighthearted chatter that had made practice such a pleasure in other years.

The mood was carried over to the locker room just before game time, and at seven-fifteen, a nervous, ill-at-ease team took the floor against Butler Academy.

The second game of the season was a disaster. None of the boys—not even Win—could do anything right. They lost the ball repeatedly, failed to score when they had a chance, and allowed an admittedly second-rate team to walk right over their defense.

In other ways, too, the Cougars showed the strain of the last few days. Boots Lohman, normally the gentlest of ballplayers, lost his temper twice and was almost thrown out of the game. A few scattered boos from the audience greeted this display of poor sportsmanship. At the end of the game, a weary, discouraged team saw from the scoreboard that they had lost by the lopsided figure of 68-39. It was the most humiliating defeat Dixboro had suffered in ten years.

On Monday morning, Travers was back doing

business at the same old stand. This time Win was singled out for attack. The last few paragraphs read:

Win Hadley, usually a 20-point man, had a miserable evening with exactly eight tallies. When a player of Hadley's potential fails to break into the two-figure column, something is wrong. And what's wrong with the fading star of the Cougars is plain for everyone to see. He can't take the double load of coaching the collection of second-rate players that call themselves the Giants and still do a first-class job of playing his Varsity position.

Open letter to Win Hadley: The time has come for you to make your choice. If you want to coach the Giants, get off the Varsity squad. If you want to play basketball, stop wasting your time with the Giants. If Tom Joyce had any sense of responsibility for his team, he'd tell you the same thing.

For some reason, Travers' article made Win angrier than he had ever been in his life. It wasn't a blind explosive sort of fury. It was more a burning desire to make Neal Travers eat his words. He walked through the remainder of Monday without remembering things too clearly.

He recalled going to school and reporting to classes. At Varsity practice he never said a word.

Even Matt Hughes couldn't get a rise out of him. Every part of Win's mind and body was pointed toward the game that night—the first one that counted for Conference standing.

The others on the squad seemed to sense that something was wrong and stayed away from him. At seven-fifteen, when Whitey Comstock announced "Time!" Win walked to the door of the gym with the fierce determination of a gladiator about to enter the arena.

He took his position on the floor and got set for the tap-up. When it came, every ounce of energy in his body was released in an overpowering surge of basketball skill. Win had never wanted to win a game so much in his life. He knew somehow that he wasn't doing it for himself, but for Tom Joyce and the others. There was only one way to show up Neal Travers and that was to prove he was wrong.

That night Dixboro basketball fans saw a game they would never forget. Time and again Win's driving play brought them to their feet with roars of approval that filled the huge gym. Win only half heard the applause. Later, his recollections of the game were vague. He remembered Boots Lohman talking to him urgently in the huddles, but the words didn't register. He remembered Tom Joyce in the half-time, lecturing quietly in the locker room. And he remembered Tom looking at him strangely, but not saying anything at the time.

The second half passed with the same dreamlike quality of confusion. Win's world was narrowed down to the ball, the opposing basket, and the players assigned to guard him.

Win was still playing, driving in for a score, when the horn sounded to end the game. He didn't realize it was all over until Boots, Matt and half the team were standing around him, pounding him on the back.

Win blinked and looked up at Matt. "We won, didn't we?"

"Won?" Matt roared. "We murdered them! We got 'em 72-59. And you scored 39 points. Man, that's a record!"

Win sighed and relaxed. Suddenly he felt extremely tired. He allowed himself to be led across the court and down the stairs to the locker room. The cheers of the fans were still echoing in his ears as he picked up a towel and headed for the showers.

On his way he passed Tom Joyce. The coach had that same strange look on his face. He approached Win and patted him on the back.

"You played quite a game," Tom said.

Win smiled briefly. "Thanks."

"Doing anything afterward?" Tom asked.

Win looked puzzled. "No. Why?"

"I'd like to talk to you. Your brother's outside

waiting, and I thought we could all drive home to-gether."

"Sure," Win said, "but—"

"I'll tell you later," Tom said as he moved away. "Right now I've got an announcement to make to the squad."

Tom Joyce moved to the center of the locker room and pounded for order. "Pipe down, fellows. I've got something to say."

The jubilant Cougars stopped their yelling and turned their attention to Tom.

"First of all," Tom said, "I want to congratulate you on a fine game. I don't mind telling you that we needed to win."

The players grinned and applauded. "But now," Tom went on, holding up his hand for silence, "I've got some unpleasant news." The room fell quiet. "I've had word from Dan Slade that he's not going to report for practice tomorrow. He told me that he can't play on this squad and that he wants to resign for the season in order to help Joe Harsh coach the Midgets. He says he feels that's more important. He handed in his suit just before game time."

Tom looked around at the stunned players and shrugged. "Well, that's it, fellows. Dan has quit the team. We'll have to go the rest of the way without him."

CHAPTER FOURTEEN

The Inside Story

SITTING IN THE FRONT SEAT of his brother's car after the game, Win felt ill-at-ease and unsure of himself. It was nothing he could put his finger on, but he had the feeling that he had done something wrong. Beside him, Walt's cigarette glowed in the darkness. Tom Joyce was in the back, searching through pockets for his pipe and tobacco pouch. Walt had parked around the corner from their home on a quiet street that was completely deserted. He was waiting for Tom to start the conversation.

At last Win heard a match strike and saw the reflection of a flare of light in the window in front of him. Finally, after he had his pipe going properly, Tom Joyce leaned forward and broke the silence.

"That was quite a performance you put on,

Win," he said. Win didn't answer. "What got you so worked up? I've never seen you like that before."

Win shrugged. "I don't know. Neal Travers, I guess."

"You wanted to win that one badly, didn't you?"

Win swung around to face Tom. "I sure did!" he cried. "I was sick and tired of the pot shots he was taking at you and the team."

Tom nodded understandingly. "I know," he soothed. "I can't blame you. But you know you played right into his hands?"

"How?"

"That was a one-man show you put on tonight. I don't know what to call it, but it certainly wasn't basketball. You were like a crazy man out there on the court. You forgot about the team—even the game. The only thing you were thinking about was Neal Travers and how to show him up. Points, points, points! That's all that mattered. Sure," Tom said hastilly as he saw Win was about to break in, "there was a reason for it. But what does it remind you of?" He paused to let his words sink in. "It reminds me of the style of basketball taught by Joe Harsh. And don't you think that Neal Travers didn't notice it! I'll bet my hat that tomorrow's column will be full of the news that Win Hadley is now playing Harsh's kind of ball. What do you think that's going to do to the team?"

Win shook his head and stared down at the seat. "I didn't realize—" he began.

Tom put his hand on Win's shoulder. "I know you didn't," he said quietly. "I just want to get you ready for what's going to happen."

Win shot a troubled glance at Tom and his brother. "Why is he doing all this?" he asked. "There must be something behind it."

Tom looked over at Walt significantly. "There is," he said. "That's why I asked your brother along. He knows the story."

Win turned to his brother. Walt rolled down the window beside him, flicked his cigarette out into the night and faced Win. "You remember the night of the School Board meeting?" he asked.

"Sure," Win said.

"You remember how Mr. Slade explained the importance of the elementary school team to everybody?

"He said it would mean new businesses moving into Dixboro."

"That's right." Walt settled back comfortably. "Now, the first thing you've got to understand, Win, is that Mr. Slade meant every word sincerely. In his own way, Owen Slade is very much concerned with the future of Dixboro. He wants to do all he can to help it grow and prosper. He hit on this idea of using an elementary school team as a way of promoting better teams and giving Dixboro better publicity. I can't say I agree with him completely, but that's not the point. Mr. Slade is convinced it's a sound program and that's enough. He's a hard man to change. He gets impatient when people don't agree with him. Okay so far?"

"I think so," Win replied. "But how does Harsh come into all this?"

"At first innocently enough. He came to town, applied for a job and got it. Then he heard his boss, Mr. Slade, talking about the new team. That gave him an idea. He knew something about basketball, so why not offer to coach the boys? He thought it was a chance to get on the good side of the boss." Walt grinned. "Boy, was he right! Just the thing Mr. Slade was looking for. After that Joe Harsh couldn't do anything wrong. The team was set up and Harsh was given the job of running it."

"That sounds simple enough," Win said. "But what started this all-out attack from Neal Travers? How did the issue of an unofficial elementary school team build up into such a snowball?"

"I'm coming to that. You've got to get the picture clear in your mind. Mr. Slade is sold on the idea of the Midgets and Joe Harsh has the responsibility of turning them into a good basketball team. Now it just so happens," Walt said, "that Harsh isn't much of a basketball coach. I checked on him. It's true that he coached a service team, but he didn't do it for long. They got rid of him before the end of the first season."

Win whistled softly. "That means—"

"That means that Joe Harsh was worried. He knew he could fool Mr. Slade and even the kids playing under him. But there was one person in Dixboro he couldn't fool."

"Tom Joyce," Win said.

"Right. Now," Walt went on, lighting a fresh cigarette, "enter Neal Travers. Remember that this whole idea started with the aim of attracting new businesses to Dixboro. Neal Travers is pretty shrewd. He knew that things might work out exactly the way Owen Slade and the Chamber of Commerce hoped. First of all, there was the question of publicity. Well, Travers could supply plenty of that through his Dixboro sports column in the *Crawford Record*. The big question mark was the team. Could they actually win games? Travers looked them over and decided they could. As a matter of fact, he was convinced they could beat any other elementary school team around— no matter how they were coached."

"You remember I told you the same thing the day we had our talk in my office," Tom said from the back. Win nodded.

"At this point," Walt continued, "Travers had

an idea. New businesses and new factories coming to Dixboro could mean money in his pocket if he played his cards carefully."

"How?" Win demanded.

"When a company wants to put up a new factory, the first thing they have to do is to buy some land. Now what kind of land do you suppose they'd look for?"

"I don't know," Win said. "They'd need a lot of open space, I guess."

"More than that. They'd want to build near a railroad line, well outside the main shopping district. Travers knew there was plenty of that kind of land around. Most of it was owned by farmers who used it for pasture. Travers thought he could get it cheap, hang on to it, then sell it when the factories moved in." Walt ground out his cigarette in the dashboard ash tray. "He didn't want to buy all the land himself, because that would attract attention. People might begin to wonder and put two and two together. So he approached Joe Harsh and suggested a partnership. Harsh," he said with a smile, "wasn't too hard to sell. They got to work quickly and began buying bits and pieces of land. Pretty soon they had sizable holdings all up and down the railroad line and, incidentally, were up to their necks in debt as a result."

Walt shifted in his seat and leaned forward.

"Now take another look at the picture. Both Harsh and Travers have committed themselves to the idea of a successful elementary school team. They face ruin if it doesn't perform properly. But that's a chance they must take. Now what happens? Tom Joyce pushes through a *second* team. That is something they haven't counted on. The second team might turn out to be better than the first."

"But so what?" Win pointed out. "Even supposing the second team was better, it still wouldn't make any difference to them. It would get the same kind of publicity and do the same job of bringing factories to Dixboro."

"You're right, except for one thing," Walt explained. "You see, whenever a company wants to build a new plant in a town, the local Chamber of Commerce appoints a committee to suggest preferred building sites. Joe Harsh asked Owen Slade for a job on that committee. And because Slade was so impressed with Harsh, he put his weight behind the appointment and Harsh got it."

"I see," Win said suddenly. "That puts Harsh in the position of being able to suggest his own land."

"You've got it," Walt nodded. "Harsh knows his job on the committee depends on Mr. Slade's opinion of him, and *that* depends on the performance of his team. If the Midgets don't do as well as Mr.

Slade expects, Harsh knows he's out. That's why the Midgets are so important. If they turn out to be flops, Harsh and Travers are finished. So now you can see," Walt concluded, "why these two men are in such a desperate situation. They're afraid that Tommy Burton's crew can beat their team."

"Well, I think they can," Win asserted.

"So do I," Walt agreed. "Harsh and Travers know a showdown is inevitable and that a game between the teams will probably be scheduled. But here's the thing—" Walt raised a finger to emphasize his words. "They want to schedule the game before Tommy Burton's team is ready. You've just started practice, right?"

Win nodded.

"Well, they've been playing for several weeks now. That gives them a considerable edge. They want to take advantage of it."

Win took a deep breath. "When," he began, "when—"

"We know that too," Walt assured him. "What's the Varsity schedule for next week?"

"We play Wednesday, Friday and Saturday," Win answered promptly. "They're all away games. We have a return match with Butler on their court. Then we play Bedloe and Parsons."

"And then?"

Win grinned. "Then comes the big one. We play Crawford on Monday night."

Walt nodded. "It'll be in Alumni Gym and the whole town will be out for that one. That's what Harsh and Travers are counting on. They want everybody to see the Midgets walk all over your Giants."

"On the night of the Crawford game?" Win asked with surprise.

"On the night of the Crawford game. It's a single game and starts at seven-thirty. Well, Harsh and Owen Slade have asked permission to schedule a double-header. They want to play your team at six o'clock. Just before the Varsity game."

"Do you think they'll get permission?"

"Sure."

"But that doesn't mean we have to play them," Win protested.

Walt disagreed. "I think you will. You see, Harsh will issue a challenge. It'll be printed in Travers' column. If you don't accept, they won't mind a bit. Then they'll have an excuse for never playing you."

"And no one will ever be able to question the fact that the Midgets are the best team around," Win said musingly.

"Or that Joe Harsh is a first-rate coach," Walt concluded.

Win nodded. "Then we'll play them," he announced firmly.

"Hold on a minute, Win." This came from Tom

Joyce. "Think what you're letting yourself in for. You'll only have a week to get ready for the game."

"We can do it," Win said confidently.

"But you'll be out of town for three of those days," Tom pointed out. "You won't be able to call practice when you're with the Varsity."

"Hmmm. All our games are at night, aren't they?"

"Yes."

"What time does the team bus leave?"

"We'll have to be off by two-thirty at the latest."

"Look here," Win said excitedly. "The rest of the team could go on without me. I can practice with the Giants until about four o'clock. Then maybe Walt could drive me to the games after he gets through with work?"

Tom turned to Walt. "How about it, Walt? You willing to act as chauffeur?"

"Sure thing," Walt replied. "Anything to put Harsh and Travers in their places."

"Of course, there'll be a lot of criticism if we do that," Tom said thoughtfully. "Travers will call it favoritism, and if we lose any of the games he'll say it was because Win was too busy to work with the Varsity."

"I wouldn't worry about that," Walt said. "No matter what happens, Travers will be blasting away at you all week long."

"I guess you're right," Tom said. He looked at Win doubtfully. "Do you think you can whip your boys into shape? It's not much time."

"I don't know," Win said grimly. "But we're sure going to try."

"Well, that's the best anyone can ask," Walt observed as he leaned over to turn on the motor.

"Wait a minute," Win said. "There's a couple of things I want to know." Walt settled back. "Did Travers or Harsh have anything to do with Dan Slade quitting the team?"

Tom and Walt exchanged glances. It was Tom who answered. "I think so. Harsh kept playing on Dan's dissatisfaction with the new style of basketball we've been using, and then later he switched over to an appeal based on loyalty. Harsh argued that Dan owed it to his father and brother to spend more time with the Midgets."

"But why?" Win asked.

Walt laughed. "Because Harsh needed Dan's help. Dan's a good player and can give him some fine tips on coaching the boys."

"And there's another reason," Tom pointed out. "By getting Dan to quit the squad, Harsh knew he was weakening the team. Don't forget, he's out after my scalp."

"I see," Win said. "Poor Dan. I bet he's a little mixed up."

Tom nodded sympathetically. "It wasn't an easy decision for him to make."

"But he made it," Walt said firmly. "And now he'll have to stick to it."

"Not necessarily," Tom answered. "I haven't removed his name from the squad roster. And I don't intend to. What was your other question, Win?"

"I wanted to know how you found out so much about Harsh and Travers."

Walt laughed a second time. "That's easy. William Madden helped us. You see, Madden publishes the *Crawford Record,* but he makes it a policy to let his writers say pretty much what they please—especially in a sports column like Travers' where it's all a matter of opinion and he feels he shouldn't impose his views. But lately Travers has been getting so vicious that Madden's been worried."

"How did you get mixed up in it?" Win demanded.

"Don't forget that I'm a member of the Chamber of Commerce. There's been some talk and Travers has done some boasting. I went to see Tom just about the same time as Bill Madden. The three of us kind of hashed things over and decided there was more to the situation than we had suspected. So we got busy and dug up a few facts."

"Well, can't something be done about it?" Win asked.

"About Travers and Harsh?" Walt said. "They haven't done anything illegal, if that's what you mean. It isn't against the law to buy property, and Travers is perfectly free to express his opinions in print."

"I see," Win said thoughtfully. "Then the only way to stop them is to win the game against the Midgets on Monday night."

Walt nodded. "And that, my boy, is your assignment. Incidentally, not a word about this to anyone. Not to Mother, or to your buddy Matt Hughes. It's all strictly confidential."

Win agreed. "Okay," he said. "I think I'll be too busy to talk much anyway."

Walt smiled. "Probably," he said. "But one word of warning. Travers and Harsh will suspect what's going on and they'll be pretty upset. As I said before, they're desperate. And if you think the stuff that Travers has been writing has been bad up to now, just wait. My guess is that he'll launch an all-out attack on you and the Giants and Tom Joyce. It'll make some pretty unpleasant reading."

"But don't let it worry you, Win," Tom said, putting a hand on Win's shoulder. "Just concentrate on the job at hand."

"I will," Win promised. "Don't worry."

CHAPTER FIFTEEN

Joe Harsh Drops a Bombshell

THE CHALLENGE CAME on Tuesday morning. It appeared, as Walt had predicted, in Neal Travers' column. "What do I do now?" Win asked Tom Joyce later that day when he ran into him at school. "How do I let him know that we're accepting?"

"The first thing I'd do," Tom suggested, "is to talk it over with Tommy Burton and the rest of the boys. They may not want to go along."

Win smiled. "I think they will."

"I do too. But I think it's only fair to consult them first. Telephone the *Crawford Record* and leave a message for Travers. Tell him that you want to consult the team and that you'll have an answer for him this afternoon."

"Will he want to see us?" Win asked anxiously.

"I imagine he will. But don't let him get under your skin. Just give him your answer. If he asks any other questions, just say 'no comment,' and tell him you have to get back to practice."

"Okay," Win agreed. "I'll do what you say."

Tommy and the others were wildly enthusiastic about the idea. "Boy!" Tommy cried, his eyes shining. "You mean we're really going to get a crack at Freddie Slade and that bunch?"

"If you want it," Win smiled.

There was a ragged cheer at this. "We can hardly wait," Tommy informed Win happily.

"Okay. But you fellows are going to have to work pretty hard. You have a lot of basketball to learn in one week."

"We'll learn it," Tommy crowed confidently.

Travers came around at two-thirty for the answer. Win had seen him before but had never spoken to him. Travers was a thin, nervous-looking man who peered suspiciously at the world through thick glasses. His narrow, pinched face seemed to twitch uncontrollably as he talked to Win.

"You think you'll have a chance, kid?" Travers asked. Win noticed that his Adam's apple bobbed up from his collar whenever he spoke.

"I think so, Mr. Travers," Win replied. "The boys have a lot of talent."

Travers grunted noncommittally. "Tommy Burton's your only real player, isn't he?" Travers said suddenly.

"I wouldn't say that," Win replied. "He's good, but there are others."

Travers laughed unpleasantly. "Come off it, kid. Without Burton you'd be dead."

Win reined in his temper and shrugged. "You're entitled to your opinion."

Travers' eyes roamed over the gym and fastened on Tommy charging in for a hook shot. Tommy feinted his guard out of his position, broke for the right-hand corner and made his shot. The ball sank through the hoop without touching the rim.

"Not bad," Travers said grudgingly. "I'd advise you to keep an eye on him, though."

"What do you mean?" Win asked.

"Don't let him get into any more trouble. He's got a bad reputation around town."

"Tommy's all right," Win said evenly.

"Maybe." Travers changed the subject. "Too bad you'll only have three days to practice this week," he said with a smile. "You'll be away with the team for three games."

When Win made no answer, Travers tried another approach. "Speaking of the Varsity, what do you think of their chances?"

Win started to reply and then checked himself. "I can't answer that, Mr. Travers. You know the rules about interviewing players."

"Dan Slade didn't seem to mind."

"Look what happened to him. He got suspended."

Travers shrugged. "Suit yourself, kid." He waved his hand breezily and turned away. "Thanks for the story. See you at the game on Monday."

Win watched him walk away and then turned back to his squad. "All right, fellows!" he shouted. "Gather 'round. We're going to set up some strategy against an all-out zone press style of play . . ."

On Wednesday, at two-thirty, the team bus left for the Butler game without Win. The young coach of the Giants was in the makeshift gym, driving his young players, when suddenly the door burst open and Travers came in. He took one look at the action on the floor and stopped in amazement. "Hey!" he shouted angrily. "Hadley! I want to talk to you!"

Win called time out and went over. "What do you want, Mr. Travers?" he asked.

The reporter was brusque. "How come you're here?" he demanded.

"Why shouldn't I be?" Win asked calmly.

"Why shouldn't you be?" Travers repeated, his voice rising in tone. "The team's already left for the Butler game!"

"I know that," Win assured him. "I'm joining them later."

Travers' jaw dropped. "But you can't! That's
. . . Who gave you permission?" he snarled.

"Coach Joyce."

Travers stood still for a moment, trying without
success to control his emotions. "He's trying to
wreck the Midgets," he said at last.

"No, he's not," Win retorted. "He's simply
making sure that the Giants get an even break
when they go into the game. I'd call it sportsmanship."

"And I'd call it favoritism!" Travers practically
yelled. He shook his fist under Win's nose and
backed away. "You won't get away with this!" he
thundered. "I'll see to that!" With that, he spun
on his heel and slammed the door behind him.

Win stared after him for a moment, then turned
back to the court. "All right!" he cried. "Let's run
through that play again. When you get the ball,
Tommy, break to your left and then hand off.
Don't do it before. By breaking over, you draw
your guard and set up a screen play. Got that?"
Tommy nodded. "Okay then, let's try it. Petey
starts the play by passing to Eddie . . ."

The Cougars lost the game that night. It was a
close affair for three quarters, but in the last eight
minutes, Butler pulled ahead and took it by a
score of 58-52.

"Just eight points more," Matt Hughes muttered on the way home. "That's all we needed. Eight miserable points. We'd have had them too if Dan Slade had been playing."

"Well, he wasn't and he won't be," Charley Bantam answered. "So we might as well forget it."

The bus pulled into Dixboro about eleven o'clock. Win went straight home, expecting to see a highly critical account of the game in Neal Travers' column the next morning.

But Travers barely mentioned the game. His column was devoted to a blasting attack on Tom Joyce and Win Hadley. He blamed Tom for allowing Win to stay behind to practice with the Giants, and called Win a quitter for following Tom's orders. It was a vicious column—probably the worst Travers had ever written.

"Don't let it upset you," Tom soothed later that day. "I was talking to your brother Walt this noon and he says that Travers is like a wild man. You've got them worried, Win. They're afraid they're going to lose that ball game."

Tommy Burton and the Giants reported for practice that day to find Win more determined than ever. "Half an hour's drill," he ordered. "You're learning the plays, but you're getting careless on fundamentals. At least twenty passes downcourt before anyone takes a shot. Let's have lots of holler now." He blew his whistle sharply. "Start her going, Eddie!" The Giants fanned over the court with a yell and began passing. . . .

"Watch out for Joe Harsh," Walt said, as he drove Win to the Bedloe game Friday night. "I've never seen a man look like that."

"What's the matter with him?" Win asked.

"He's at the end of his rope. He'll do anything to keep you from winning on Monday."

Win settled back easily. "What can he do, Walt? There's only a couple of days left."

"I don't know," Walt admitted. He pushed down on the accelerator and drove the car forward. "I only wish I did."

The Bedloe game was a thriller from start to finish. Bedloe was in the Conference and was in there trying every second, but Boots Lohman and Tony Parsons had a perfect night. The two veterans seemed to be able to read each other's minds. The brilliance of their play carried Dixboro through the game and to a comfortable victory. Final score was 64-51. Boots hit the target for 22 points and Tony rang the bell for 27. Together, they played the entire game and were as solid on defense as they were deadly in offense.

It was a cheerful bus ride back to Dixboro.

"Not bad!" Matt exulted. "Maybe we've lost a couple, but they haven't been to Conference teams."

"Right!" Teddy Scholari cheered. "We've got a two–nothing Conference record."

"Wait until Monday night," Gabby Windham put in. "We've got Crawford to face."

"We'll take 'em easy," was Teddy Scholari's confident opinion.

"Oh yeah?" Ed Walsh challenged. "Without Dan Slade?"

The noise in the bus quieted considerably.

"We're going to work on the fast break today," Win told his squad Saturday morning. "Here's the way we'll play it." He dragged out a blackboard and began to sketch in the players and their positions. The Giants sat cross-legged on the floor of the gym and concentrated on Win's words. . . .

"Take it easy, Win," Walt advised his brother on Saturday night. "You're pacing back and forth like a caged lion."

Win flashed him a grin. "That's the way I feel."

"Only two more days," Walt said.

"I know. But it seems forever."

"Think your boys are ready?"

Win nodded. "It's amazing what they've done in a week."

"You know it's impossible to get tickets for that game," Walt told him.

"The more the merrier," Win said happily. "How are Harsh and Travers holding up?"

"I haven't seen Harsh lately, but Travers looks worried. Incidentally, Win, have you told your boys to watch out for rough stuff?"

"How do you mean?"

"Oh, you know the old business. Try to get the other team so mad they'll make mistakes. Maybe even start a fight and get thrown out of the game."

"Oh, sure," Win said. "I've warned them all. Especially Tommy. He's got a hot temper, but I've had a long talk with him."

"I bet they'll try to pour it on Tommy pretty thick," Walt predicted. "I hope he can take it without blowing his stack."

Win smiled. "We've made an agreement," he said. "Whenever Tommy gets mad, he's promised to look over at the bench."

"Good." Walt hauled himself out of his chair. "Come on, boy. Let's get moving. You've got a game of your own to play tonight."

"Right."

Win played like a fireball in the Parsons game, breaking through their defense time and again to register for Dixboro. But the team as a whole was sluggish and a little tired from three road games in quick succession. They failed to respond to Win's drive and allowed Parsons to gain a commanding lead in the third quarter. Despite his 29 points, Win couldn't shake the Cougars out of their depression. Parsons took it handily, 69–54.

Sitting in the back of the silent bus on the way home, Tom Joyce shook his head despondently. The team just wasn't going anywhere. They'd win one and then lose two. Tom had learned a long time ago that it was impossible to win them all. But he also knew that a good team didn't let defeat hurt them the way this team did. Tom sighed and stared out the window. They needed Dan Slade. Even more, they needed the feeling of being a team. That was the trouble. There were fifteen boys in the bus and they all played together. But they didn't do it as a team. There wasn't that spirit —that special something that was so essential for a squad of championship caliber. Actually, that was the most important thing of all, Tom decided. Win or lose, it made no difference, as long as the boys felt they were part of a team. That was the whole problem. Well, maybe the game on Monday night would give him the answer. He wondered idly how good Tommy Burton really was. He'd know soon enough. . . .

It was five-thirty. Upstairs the gym was packed to the roof. Down below, in the visitors' locker room, Tommy Burton and the Giants were nervously suiting up. They wore old cast-off uniforms that had once belonged to the freshman squad but had since been discarded. Most of the trunks were too big, and here and there the shirts had holes in them. But at least they were all the same color and each uniform had a number sewn on the back.

"How do you feel, Tommy?" Win asked, doing his best to keep his voice casual.

Tommy looked at him seriously, his eyes wide as saucers. "Butterflies," he announced nervously. "Here in my stomach."

"Don't worry about it," Win assured him. "Everybody gets them."

Tommy nodded unhappily. "I wish we'd get going," he said nervously.

"Stretch out on the bench," Win advised. "It'll help you relax. By the way," he said, "how come you were late tonight?"

"I wasn't late," Tommy explained. "I got here before anybody else. It was just that I was in the wrong locker room. I didn't know they'd be giving us the visitors' space."

"Okay." Win smiled. "Take it easy." He moved off to say a word or two to the other boys. As he got to the end of the row of lockers, he looked up at the clock. Twenty of six. Almost time. He took a deep breath and turned down the next row.

That was when the door burst open to let in what looked like a mob of people. Win got a glimpse of Dan Slade and his father. Behind them came Joe Harsh, looking smug and satisfied, with Neal Travers at his elbow. Bringing up the rear came Tom Joyce, Mr. Anson, the high school principal, and William Madden, publisher of the *Crawford Record*. All of them looked grave and serious.

Owen Slade shouldered his way down the stairs and stared around angrily. He caught sight of Tommy Burton lying down in front of his locker and strode over to the boy.

"There he is!" he shouted. "That's the one who stole the money out of Dan's locker."

"Now wait a minute," Tom said, pulling up beside him. "Let's not be hasty. We don't know anything for certain."

"Oh, yes, we do!" Mr. Slade said. "He was seen. He was seen taking the wallet out of Dan's trousers."

"By whom?" Tom demanded. "Who saw him?"

Owen Slade pointed over to Joe Harsh. "He saw him. With his own eyes. Less than three quarters of an hour ago."

There was a gasp of astonishment and the locker room suddenly became quiet. Mr. Slade turned indignantly to Mr. Anson. "I demand that this boy be taken into custody. At once."

In the stunned silence that followed, Tommy got shakily to his feet and looked at Win pleadingly. His face was drained of all color and there was a frightened, hunted look in his eyes.

CHAPTER SIXTEEN

Overtime Upset

IN THE BURST OF CONFUSION that followed Mr. Slade's accusation, Tom Joyce kept his head. "Quiet!" he shouted firmly. "Let's have it quiet here!" As the room simmered down, he turned to Owen Slade. "We'll start from the beginning," he said. "I take it that your son is missing his wallet?"

Joe Harsh interrupted with a short laugh. "Oh, the wallet's not missing," he said. "We know perfectly well where it is. That young hoodlum—" he pointed a finger at Tommy. "He's got it."

"We'll get to that later. Dan, have you lost your wallet?"

Dan stepped forward. "Yes, sir."

"When did you first miss it?"

"When I came to the locker room to change for the game, I hung up my trousers and pulled on an

181

old pair of slacks. Then I waited for my brother and the rest of the Midgets."

"Were you in the locker room all the time?"

"No, sir. I went out into the hallway for a little fresh air."

"And when you came back was your brother there?"

"Yes, he had arrived, and so had some of the other fellows on the team."

"Then what happened?"

"About twenty minutes ago, I went to my locker for a stick of chewing gum. I reached into my trousers and noticed my wallet was gone."

"You're sure you had left it there?"

"Positive."

"When do you think it was taken?"

"During the time I went out into the hallway. That was the only chance. The room was beginning to fill up when I got back."

"What makes you think it was Tommy Burton?"

Dan hesitated. "Well, sir, when I got back, Tommy was just leaving."

"Your locker room?"

"Yes, sir. He told me he had gotten mixed up and had reported to the wrong dressing area."

"That's right!" Win interrupted eagerly. "That's just what Tommy told me—"

"All right now, you quiet down, too," Tom told

Win. "We'll hear your side of it in a minute." He turned back to Dan. "What did you do after you found your wallet was gone?"

"I didn't know what to do. I was wandering around trying to make up my mind and then I saw Mr. Harsh. I told him what had happened and he said he had seen Tommy Burton go into my locker and take my wallet. That's all I know."

Tom swung around to face Joe Harsh. "Is that true?" he asked.

Harsh licked his lips and nodded. "That's right," he said with a grin. "I caught the kid red-handed."

"That's a lie!" Tommy broke out. "I never—"

"All right, Tommy," Tom Joyce said gently. "Look at me." The boy raised a frightened face. "Did you steal Dan Slade's wallet?"

Tommy shook his head. "No, sir."

"You're quite sure?"

"Oh, no, sir. I wouldn't do a thing like that!"

There was an ugly laugh from Harsh. "The boy's a liar. He's done it before."

Tom almost lost his temper. "That'll be enough!" he cried. Harsh looked surprised but backed away. Tom went over to Tommy and sat down beside him. "Look, Tommy, we're going to have to search your locker. If you haven't taken the wallet, there's nothing to be worried about."

"I don't mind," Tommy said.

"Of course, he doesn't mind," Harsh bleated. "You don't suppose he's still got it, do you? He's hidden it someplace." He moved forward and stood facing Tom Joyce. "Look, I'm getting tired of this. I tell you I saw that kid take Dan's wallet. Now it's my word against his, and you know the kind of record he has." He turned to Principal Anson for support. "I demand that he be barred from further participation in Dixboro athletics. The boy should be taken down to police headquarters and made a lesson of. That's all there is to it. He stole the wallet!"

The next words froze everyone in the room into attitudes of disbelief. "Oh, no, he didn't," came a voice from the rear. "Nobody stole it."

Several dozen eyes swiveled to find the speaker. It was Whitey Comstock, Dixboro's trainer, who came forward. Silently the crowd parted to give him room.

"Most of you probably know," he began, "that on nights when games are scheduled in the gym I usually come a little early to open the place up and hang out towels and get my equipment all ready. Well, I did it tonight, same's any other game. I got here a little before five, put everything in order and went back to my office in back of the locker room." He grinned shyly. "It ain't much more'n a broom closet, but I call it my office. I was in there, waiting for the fellows to show up—I might have dozed off a little—when all of a sudden I heard a noise. I got up to take a look and saw Dan Slade had come in early to change. I saw him hang up his trousers in his locker and I saw something fall out of his pocket. It was his wallet. I yelled out, but Dan didn't hear, I guess. Anyway, he didn't stop, so I went over and picked it up to hold for him." Whitey fumbled in his pocket and came up with a plain black leather wallet. "This what you're looking for?" he asked mildly.

There was a gasp of astonishment from the crowd. Dan stepped forward with a puzzled look on his face. He reached out for the wallet and examined it carefully.

"Is it yours?" Tom asked quietly.

Dan nodded. "Yes, that's it," he said. "But how . . . ?"

"Take a look inside," Tom ordered. "See if anything's missing."

Dan thumbed through the contents. "Everything's here," he announced at last.

"And so," Tom said triumphantly, "it seems that Tommy Burton didn't steal Dan's wallet." He turned to face Mr. Slade. "Wouldn't you agree?"

"Yes, but . . ." Mr. Slade stammered. "But why did—"

"Why did Joe Harsh say he had?" Tom finished for him. He swung around in Harsh's direction. "Suppose *you* answer that?"

The coach of the Midgets had gone deathly pale. He looked around nervously and began to edge toward the door. "I'll explain everything later," he muttered weakly.

"You'll explain it now!" Mr. Slade thundered. "You can't make a false accusation of theft against an innocent boy and then say you won't explain!"

Harsh lifted one arm as if he were trying to ward off Mr. Slade's anger. "I—It's a long story." He turned and started for the steps. "I'm upset right now. I'll come down and talk to you in the morning."

Mr. Slade made a motion to stop Harsh, but Tom Joyce grabbed his arm. "Let him go," he advised. "He can't go very far in one night."

Mr. Slade looked around with a bewildered stare. "Will someone please tell me what's going on? Why did Harsh say that the boy stole Dan's wallet?"

"Because he wanted to discredit Tommy Burton. He wanted to frame him."

"But why?" Mr. Slade insisted.

"Harsh wanted to keep Tommy from playing tonight. When he heard that Dan had lost his wallet, he saw a chance to create a scene. He knew the charge wouldn't stick, but he hoped that it would last long enough to keep Tommy out of the game. It was a dirty trick and it almost worked."

Mr. Slade threw up his hands in despair. "I still don't understand. It seems that something's going on that I don't know about."

"There is," Tom said. He glanced up at the clock. "But it's almost game time. Supposing I tell you later."

"It involves Harsh, I suppose?" Mr. Slade said grimly.

"Oh yes. And Neal Travers, too."

Travers, who had been trying to slip away through the crowd, stopped and paled noticeably. "Me?" he cried. "I didn't do anything!"

Mr. Madden, the publisher of the *Crawford Record,* stepped forward.

"Legally you didn't commit any crime," he said. "But you did use your position on my newspaper for personal gain. And you did it irresponsibly. A newspaper," Mr. Madden went on, "has a public service to perform, and a newspaperman carries the burden of that trust. You violated public confidence, Travers, and because of that, I'm firing you. Don't bother covering tonight's game. I haven't forgotten how to write a story. I'll do it. You're through."

He turned abruptly and walked over to Tom

Joyce. "What do you say we get this show on the road? It's nearly six."

Tom looked over at Tommy and the Giants. "You fellows still feel like playing?" he asked. "I wouldn't blame you if you wanted to call it off."

Tommy stepped forward firmly. "No, sir!" he said. "We'll go through with it. We want to get up there and lick the spots off them!"

"And you will, too!" Win said proudly.

The game between the Midgets and the Giants was a one-sided affair. Three thousand amazed and cheering fans saw Tommy and his friends play with superb teamwork while Freddie and the Midgets ran after the ball with an every-man-for-himself attitude. The final score was 48-19.

After the game was over, during the intermission before the Crawford game, Dan Slade walked across the locker-room floor to Win's bench. He looked more serious than Win had ever seen him. "Win," Dan said quietly, "I want to apologize. I've been a first-class dope."

Win, who knew how much the effort had cost Dan, held out his hand without a word. The two boys looked at each other for a moment, and then Win broke into a smile. "Let's forget it, Dan."

Dan tried a thin smile and nodded. "Okay." He turned to go and then came back. "Good luck tonight, Win. I'll be rooting for you and the whole team."

Win looked at him in surprise. "What do you mean? Good luck yourself!"

It was Dan's turn to show astonishment. "I'm not playing. I threw myself off the team. Remember?" he said bitterly.

Win laughed and clapped him on the back. "Maybe you'd better talk to the coach. All I know is he never took you off the squad roster."

Dan took a step forward. "You mean it?" he asked excitedly. "You're—you're not kidding?"

"Ask him and see," Win answered, laughing.

Win watched while Dan threaded his way through the locker room to where Coach Joyce was standing with Whitey. There was a short discussion which ended with Tom giving Dan a mighty wallop that sent him flying back.

"Hey, you were right! I'm in! What do you know about that?"

"Well, don't just stand there. Get dressed, idiot."

And Dan started to whirl clothes off and on like a quick-change artist.

Up in the stands, Mr. Slade was busy with his thoughts. The story he had just heard had opened his eyes. Tom Joyce was okay. There was another fellow who was all right, too. His name was

Tommy Burton. Mr. Slade promised himself to go over and shake Tommy's hand after the game. "Maybe," he muttered, "just maybe he won't hold any grudge against me!" He sighed and shook his head. "I sure hope so."

"Hey, Gabby! How many points you going to score?"

"A hundred and seventy-eight, natch!"

"Yay for Gabby!" A lusty cheer followed.

"Anyone going to the Malt Shop after?" The question was hurled across the room by Red Mc-Ginley.

"Sure!" came an answering roar.

"We'll take the place over!"

"For a victory celebration!"

"That's the stuff!"

"Quiet!" a voice bawled. "Here comes the coach!"

Tom Joyce threaded his way through the players and smiled. "Not much time left, fellows. As you know, there's been some excitement tonight." A burst of laughter greeted this remark. "So we're a little behind schedule. Anyway, there's not much I can tell you. You've played Crawford before and it's just about the same bunch as last season. The only thing I can say is—Good Luck!" He looked up at the clock. "All set?" The players nodded and

Tom led the way up the stairs and paused by the double doors. On the stroke of seven-fifteen, he threw them open. "Let's go, Dixboro!" he yelled.

The Cougars loosed a throaty roar and surged out on the court. Tom held back for a moment and watched them take their warm-up shots. It was an entirely different team. It was— He was groping for the word when Whitey Comstock sidled up behind him.

"They look pretty good," Whitey said proudly, as he peered over Tom's shoulder.

Tom nodded.

"I didn't think we were going to have a team this year," Whitey went on. "In fact, I'd just about given them up." He sighed. "But I should have known better. They came through just like champions."

"You upset about being wrong?" Tom asked with a smile.

"Heck, no!" Whitey looked at him and snapped his fingers. "That's just what it was," he said. "I had those boys tapped as a bunch of losers. But they made it. In my book, that's an upset."

"About time, too," Tom said.

"Overtime," Whitey added. "Yes, sir," he mused. "A regular overtime upset."

Then suddenly Tom thought of the word he had been looking for. The Dixboro Varsity was dif-

ferent because now it was a team. Win, lose or
draw, they were a team. No misfits. Everybody
working and pulling together. Tonight didn't matter. Crawford didn't matter. Most of the season
still stretched ahead. It was going to be a wonderful year after all.

Up in the stands, the band blared out the Dixboro team song. Tom turned and put his arm
around Whitey's shoulder. "Come on, old-timer.
Let's go on out there."

As they stepped into the brilliantly lighted gymnasium playing area, the fans rose to their feet and
greeted them with a thunderous ovation. The Dixboro basketball season was well under way.